MORAG'S FLYING FORTRESS

'Do you like this?' asked Vicky at four o'clock.

'Yes.'

She said, between oral caresses, 'I've only had two men since I came to London. One of those was John.'

'All right, let's try again.'

Ragusson sent her, of course. By the morning – I realized afterwards – this dumb, pretty, sexy cave girl knew all about my bereavement, where Sandra works in Brussels, about how she fell in love, was conned, betrayed me, whichever way you care to look at it; about Jacques Conte. By the morning Vicky knew more than you do at the moment. I was being set up. We are coming towards the beginning of the story.

Jack Trevor Story

Morag's
Flying Fortress

Arrow Books

Arrow Books Limited
3 Fitzroy Square, London W I P 6JD

An imprint of the Hutchinson Publishing Group

London Melbourne Sydney Auckland
Wellington Johannesburg and agencies
throughout the world

First published by Hutchinson 1976
Arrow edition 1979
© Jack Trevor Story 1976

Made and printed in Great Britain
by The Anchor Press Ltd
Tiptree, Essex

ISBN 0 09 919300 0

'How strange, to have failed as a social creature —
even criminals do not fail that way — they are the
law's Loyal Opposition, so to speak. But the insane
are always mere guests on earth, eternal strangers
carrying around broken decalogues that they
cannot read.'

F. Scott Fitzgerald

I

It was one of those mornings when everything rhymes.

It's not that all the troubles and confusions and uncertainties are not still there. What you've got to do is wake up with amnesia. Your mind is untangled. The paths that kept going sideways now lie right ahead, the late autumn flowers blend with simple colours, a breeze presses comfortably chill on the skin of your face and neck, your hair stirs tangibly on your scalp. Between the high villas and the high trees the sun hangs in a smoke-blue void without shining, as comfortable to look at with your clear eye as a frosted hundred-watt lamp. Order has come out of chaos, you are again a part of the universe and alive. Very likely there will be more confusions by lunchtime but you will not get caught up in them because you are in control again. Yesterday's madness has gone.

Something had happened to bring about this state of calm. It didn't happen all at once. It was something followed by a number of other things. At fifty-six your life runs in ruts; it would take some time to notice that you're dead. You can get a kick up the arse, followed by a bang on the head and a sharp push in the psyche, and still you stay in the rut. Then one morning you wake up and there's a new world and a new you and everything rhymes. What has happened is metaphysical; it's between your deep subconscious and the universe.

In any case, I don't think that one woman is all that important. I am talking now from this bright morning of strength and not from the eighteen months of purgatory. There would be backslidings, but like the familiar sudden pain that you know finally goes, it would never be as bad again, it would never seem fatal again; I would know that I was going to live.

If you have lost somebody, through death or desertion, you will understand something of this. Ordinary living takes ordinary nerve. If you lose your nerve you become a social statistic: mentally sick or unemployed, suicidee, drop-out, family burden, recluse or, what is worse, someone apparently normal but obsessed. 'She's a bit odd and rather pathetic but you'll like her,' they used to say about one of mother's sisters who lost her young man in the First World War. She always appeared to be waiting patiently for a bus that never came. And one of the things she did when she visited was clean meticulously the black bottoms of all the saucepans and kettles in the house. My earliest memory is of Aunt Ruth sitting at the kitchen table, still with her hat on, using that pink brick powder that used to make such a mess in the nineteen-twenties.

Having an Aunt Ruth among your family memories helps you to recover from all sorts of things.

Rhyme and chime, then; the church bells with the traffic with a distant ambulance bleat with a dog barking with the long slow grind of low gears that turns out to be the road-sweeper as I come within sight of the tube station. It's early yet and the sun is in the air, rather than in the sky, and it's in people's faces, the early shoppers. There's a steady queue of London-bound traffic at the lights, but locally we're hardly awake. I bought a paper.

'No change yet, sir. Have you got the exact money?'

There's a comradeship at this hour which I'm not usually up to share. Girls like Sandra walked into the station ahead of me, for it was secretary time. I spent the morning shopping in Oxford Street, Soho and the Strand and by twelve-thirty found the Lamb public house in Covent Garden and met a man I have not seen for twenty years. This narrative starts here, where it does, on that particular day, because of this reunion. Because I was meeting someone who knew me on the other side of the abyss. The place was lunch-hour crowded and there was nowhere to put my shopping, three coloured bags full of all the things Sandra had wanted me to wear and I never would.

'Alec Ranger.'

That's me; Geoffrey was standing by the bar. He was the chap I had just looked at and failed to recognize. We smiled at each other; two middle-aged versions of the chums we had been at Poly in 1952. We might now be our own fathers. Amid the hubbub we drank beer and tried to make our chat sound friendly and familiar, turned twenty years into a few casual clichés. I am now a consultant freelance sales engineer in electronic automation; Geoffrey has an editorial job with a technical publisher.

'I thought we might have a drink at Danny's,' he said.

Following Geoffrey out through the crowd I was able to examine him. He was more recognizable from the back and I felt a certain warmth for him, as you would towards a fellow survivor. He has a thick scrubbing brush of grey hair now and thick sideboards as a concession to the seventies; otherwise Geoffrey had turned out straight. He still wore suits and ties, his trousers were not flared; and worse, from my own pre-judiced point of view, he wore one of those little overcoats with a fringe of wool or fur around the collar. I've always had the lowest opinion of people who frame their faces, either with fur or by turning up the back of the collar or pulling their shirt collar outside to be seen over a jumper or jacket. The vain and childlike Hawaiians do the same thing with flowers; I think it's called a laiti.

'This is a wine bar,' he said, as we stood outside Danny's in King Street. 'Do you drink wine?'

He gave me the impression that he considered wine drinking was superior; occasionally he cleared his throat, nervously. Altogether, old Geoff has not turned out too well. He lives in Wembley and drives a Cortina. There are better things to be said about him; and also worse. He was genuinely pleased to see me; this must be a good thing. 'I've often thought about people like you,' he said at one stage. 'You know, people you used to know. You wonder what's happening to them. We never keep in touch, do we? We pass each other by in life.

When you get older you regret it. I need friends now. That's why I rang you, really. It wasn't just the book.'

I'd sent his firm a manuscript about industrial recorders and controllers. I happen to know a lot about such things. I thought it would be nice to have a textbook published; perhaps a standard reader that would go on selling to generations of students, like Ternan's *Radio Communication*. Besides, it would improve my standing with the company and increase my prestige at college – I teach night classes.

'I don't think our firm will take it,' Geoffrey told me, regretfully, before that sunny day was over. 'They think it's already covered. There won't be a demand.'

'Of course there's a demand,' I said. 'That practical detailed aspect hasn't been covered at all. There's servo mechanisms, there's automation integrated with maths and sociology – nobody's dangled glass electrodes down lavatories or shown how to crack a calcium shell off a coated antimony electrode or control a grain hopper from dielectric changes in wet seed – '

I stopped talking because he was laughing; he looked much more like his old twenty-five-year-old self when he laughed. 'That's what I wanted from you,' he explained. 'That should be on the blurb. I'll get that on before I show it to Ragusson – I think he'll take it.'

'I thought you said he'd rejected it?'

'I lied,' Geoffrey said. 'I wanted it in a nutshell – nobody wants to wade through a bloody book.'

'You lazy sod,' I said.

We were suddenly back at the Poly again and laughing.

I don't know whether you ever remember somebody from the distant past entirely by one remark. This is how Geoffrey has survived in my cluttered head; through twenty years of old marriage, job shifting, career changing, watching children grow into civil servants, travelling Europe; through my five glorious years with Sandra and through the hell after she went. When the telephone rang and I picked it up and a voice said: 'Guess who this is. . . .' Well no, that's badly presented, I didn't know who the hell it was though it stirred something. When he said it was Geoffrey Neasden – 'remember the Poly' – then I remembered his comment about rape. It had come out of the blue while we were eating canteen bread and beef dripping before classes. The way somebody will mention something you don't even expect them to be aware of or interested in.

'What do you think of this?' he had said, showing me an October 1953 *Evening News* headline. It was about a rape case; some man had gone to prison for five years. 'He deserves it,' I said. It takes two to make love. Rape seemed to me then to be the worst kind of violation of a woman's privacy and rights. 'Shit,' Geoffrey said. 'Come off it, Alec. How many girls would you like to rape? Rape is natural. If we were absolutely honest about our impulses we'd spring on top of women and rip their clothes off all the time.' I said to him : 'Remind me not to take you home to meet my daughters and my wife. . . .'

Typical Poly chat, really; I hear it at night classes any night of the week. Who wants to talk about electricity and magnetism? Anyway, that's the only way in which Geoffrey Neasden had survived in my mind for all this time. We were heading for the same kind of careers at the time. Geoffrey always wanted to write and had had one short story in the *Evening News*; he had compromised and become a technical writer. We circulated among the same kind of companies : Siemens, BICC, Standard Telephones, Marconi, Western-Electric, GEC and so on. You're inclined to circulate at that age and stage, seeking advantages of job and money, always bumping into the same people, meeting underlings as bosses, bosses as underlings, spotting your old friends at trade shows, conventions, exhibitions, seeing each other's articles or post-appointments in journal and trade press (I think I saw two of Geoffrey's articles in *Electronics* in those twenty years, for instance) and then it's all over.

You find your niche and never see old friends again.

'We've just got a manuscript in from you,' Geoffrey had told me, over the telephone. ' "Industrial Recording and Control in Batch and Continuous Processes" by Alec Ranger, AMIEE – could that be you?'

'Good God. That's a coincidence. What are you doing there?' It was exactly the sort of job I would expect him to have.

'Why don't we meet for lunch? On the firm? My firm, I mean. I'm chief editor, after all – just to impress you. Do you know the Lamb . . . ?'

On the plus side, then, Geoffrey still admired me. He had admired me in those young days. For my attitudes, I think. He was going to be a worrier and I wasn't. You always get a certain amount of envy from worriers. They are always seeing the worst ahead of them. They're hard-up while they're still rich, dead when they're still well. I had a wife and kids on practically nothing while he was still terrified of committing himself with Joyce. She was a secretary at the Poly and lived on Canvey Island and had a ghastly train journey home every night. I made love to her in the freezing cold at Waterloo Station several times, waiting for her last train. Geoffrey was in love with her and buying her flowers and getting nothing. He's the kind that lives with his parents for fear there might be something worse.

'Do you still play the clarinet?' Geoffrey suddenly asked, as if perhaps a bit bored with the present me and anxious to be certain he'd got the right chap. I was in the middle of some anecdote demonstrating my present sophisticated and successful way of life. He then said: 'Joyce always thought you'd finish up with your own band.' At my blank look he added: 'My wife. You remember Joyce. She worked at the Poly.' He married her!

'Good heavens. Did you marry Joyce?' This sounded like, of all of us who could have done, you did it; like emptying the dustbins, in other words. So I said: 'Tell me what she looked like.'

'She's dead now,' he said, as if to save a lengthy and pointless duel.

'Oh dear. I am sorry, Geoffrey . . .'

I was relieved. Am I a Christian or a monster? The last time I heard from Joyce she was pregnant and I was the father.

I couldn't do anything to help because by that time I had family troubles of my own. Mary was having a nervous breakdown and a baby at about the same time (Raymond is now a tax personnel officer at Somerset House), we were out of work, out of money, half out of our flat. I remember a telephone call when Joyce was looking for an abortionist and I remember a despairing postcard that Mary found.

'For God's sake help me. I don't want to see you. I just want some money. J.'

Luckily she had not put my name on it and I was able to deny it was meant for me. That was the last I heard of Joyce. It was on my conscience for a long time, otherwise I wouldn't be remembering it now. I did as bad or worse to Mary in the end, and to Barbara, and I've done as bad or worse to other women. When Sandra left me last year instead of me leaving her I had it coming.

'That's Mr Ragusson just came in,' Geoffrey said. 'I'll introduce you in a minute.' My despicable mind clocked up the 'Mr' and the little nervous cough and it wasn't on the plus side. Looking at Ragusson you were looking at the Mafia, dark glasses and all. He didn't have to see you until he came over to you. If you were trying to guess his line you would never guess that he published journals like *Electronics in Industry, Commerce and Medicine* or textbooks like the one that I wanted to bring out. What we forget is that money is money and that Covent Garden and Bloomsbury and Soho are next door to each other. There are doctors and surgeons in University College Hospital and barristers in the Temple whom you wouldn't leave alone with your sister. Not on sight, that is. There are also gangsters, hoods, killers, ponces, racketeers in Soho that can play Father Christmas without a disguise.

'Don't forget we've had lunch.' Geoffrey's anxious little smile probed at me; friend or foe, stranger or old friend. I could see now how he had changed. He was full of money worries. His throat clearings until I'd accepted beer and not asked for scotch. Smoking only Freeman's cigarettes. Now fiddling on expenses. 'If he asks. You haven't got any restaurant bills, have you?' I don't keep restaurant bills. 'They're like gold dust. I've got an arrangement with one of the waiters here. You didn't want lunch, did you?'

It only now occurred to him that lunch would have been reasonable, that he had suggested it. I told him that I never ate midday. In fact I'm just getting used to food again. For three months after Sandra fell in love with somebody else I starved from thirteen stone down to eleven; now appetites were returning. Soon I would want a woman.

'Mr Neasden?' The girl behind the bar was leaning in on us. This one for instance. I could enjoy her without any involvement, like pink ice-cream. Danny's Cave, if you don't know it, is all white stucco marzipan and chi-chi; you go through white rocky cavities like Noddy in Toyland, you get served through a crevice by puppet girls in pink shiny dresses with their nipples pushing through. You probably have to wind them up for sexual intercourse. She said: 'Mr Ragusson wants to buy you two gentlemen a drink.'

'Oh? Ah! Ahem!' said Geoffrey, just by way of a delighted, excited preliminary. It is really pitiful what happens to people. You'd never think he once dragged me up a steep slate roof at the Polytechnic; we lay there smoking hash and gazing over London, lords of the stars. 'Have a large scotch,' he said now, furtively. 'Then I can charge him for three more. Well, he saves it on tax.'

'Scotch?' said the girl. Danny's is a wine bar that sells spirits.

I declined; I'm trying to dry out now. I was more interested in the girl than the drink. Her name is Vicky and she lives in Belsize Park and I have since slept with her a few times. I don't want to hang this story on any sexual pegs because Sandra is still the only woman for me. I was not cured of her, you understand; only cured of doing nothing about getting her back. She was going to have to want me and to want our dull old London art-belt life together again.

Ragusson had half turned to acknowledge our indebtedness for the drinks. He was talking to a dark-visaged man who had been watching me as if maybe Ragusson was talking about me. Geoffrey said he was a Belgian named Tonne and he did not know much else about him. I got the impression that Geoffrey was not in Ragusson's confidence and I'm not surprised. When you get to cheating your employer on expenses the relationship has no value on either side. I mean why waste your life in a job that only gives you money? We shall find out.

Geoffrey was clearing his throat again. It gave what he was about to say an air of mystery. 'You travel abroad quite a lot, then, Alec?' But for the throat clearing I might have thought he was making conversation. Geoffrey Neasden is the last person to try and pass off leading questions as trivialia. Yes, I have come out of my homely shell and I do sell instrumentation on the Continent. But I had not mentioned it.

'It's in your manuscript,' he explained. 'You're talking about finding new applications for the electro-encephalograph. Brain recordings.' I remembered it well. 'You mention a neurological laboratory in Poland. Sounds interesting.'

'I don't pretend to understand what they're doing. Medically, I mean,' I told him.

'Mr Ragusson thought that was very interesting,' Geoffrey said. I said: 'I thought you haven't given him the book yet?' Geoffrey said: 'I told him about it. About you. Your background and so on. I hope you don't mind. Helps to give you a build-up. Well –' he cleared his throat again ' – and me in a way. I told him you sent the book to us because of me. Old pals' act and so on. I mean as publishers we're not in the top three. We're inclined to get rejects. Second bests, perhaps. I told him you gave us first choice.'

I said: 'I hope you haven't misled him. My book's about automatic process control. Medical equipment is a side-issue. There was a drug-intake problem at the Danzig Institute. They were using brain voltage to control it. I don't know why or how. We had to produce a certain minimum galvanometer deflection from each brain electrode.'

Geoffrey said: 'It would be interesting to know what they're doing.'

'Not to me it wouldn't. Gives me the bloody shivers.'

Geoffrey laughed, then explained why. 'You haven't

changed very much, Alec. Everything used to give you the bloody shivers. Did you ever get that boat?'

He's got a good memory. When it came to anything outside that rut I mentioned earlier, anything dangerous, adventurous; no, I'm over-stating it to save face; when it comes to anything rather uncomfortable, slightly risky, anything involving un-known factors, then Alec Ranger, AMIEE, is the world's biggest yellow-bellied coward. Sandra's new boy-friend has got a boat. He's got most of the things I promised her all the five years we were together.

'Remember the night I took you on the Poly roof?' he said then. I remembered then what he put me through that night; and how much I hated him afterwards. Then as the past re-created itself in the drink, he said: 'How did you come down today?' I told him I came by tube. 'Oh? Ahem. Good,' said Geoffrey. In his day I couldn't travel underground, I had never flown, I wouldn't ride on the back of his scooter. I think he was finding me improved, however I found him.

'Mr Ragusson's coming over. Don't forget we've had lunch.'

'Did you enjoy your expensive lunch, Mr Ranger?' were Ragusson's first words, knowing that it had been the subject of his editor's last warning. It established for me – as it was meant to do – that Ragusson was nobody's fool. 'Editor!' he said to Geoffrey, looking at a non-existent watch: 'Edit!' Geoffrey took a second to cotton on, then with a slight embar-rassment he said: 'Oh! Ahem! Yes, my goodness.' He finished his drink at one gulp and put half of it down his sheepskin collar.

Ragusson watched all this, implacably, then said to me: 'Let me get you a brandy, Mr Ranger?' I stopped Geoffrey's obedient rush back to work by holding his shoulder. 'See you when you've come to a decision?' 'Eh?' he said, knowing that he took no decisions. 'Oh, the book. Yes. Ahem. Capital!' And he ran out through the cave door into the hard world.

Ragusson stood and shook for a moment and I realized that he was laughing at his slave; he was too well mannered to pass any comment, however. I took a lemonade shandy this time.

'You are not a drinking man?' he asked.

'Not now.'

'You drank too much at one time?'

'Yes.'

'Then you have a hidden tragedy.'

'Yes.'

It remained hidden while we drank our drinks. In a moment he said: 'Do you sing?' I said: 'No.' 'Pity,' he said. 'I'd rather you sang than whistled.' I have this bad habit of bridging a hiatus with a tooth whistle. By this time I could appreciate that Mr Ragusson was a comedian. I apologized. He put on a Mexican voice: 'Is all right, is okay. I let you into my secret, Mr Ranger. I fart.' I was suddenly aware of the most appalling smell. The beautiful Vicky was looking at me through the bar crevice, her face horrified. She held her breath and walked the length of the bar, flapping a wiping-up cloth.

'That girl has got the biggest tits in Covent Garden,' Ragusson said, with the experience of a big man in a small world.

I said: 'What country is Ragusson?'

'Norway,' he said. 'Viking country. My friends call me a Fiking Publisher. Trouble is I can't wear my horns under a bowler hat. Tell me about your book.'

I told him less than he knew already and he did not appear to be listening. He appeared to be watching the man he had just been talking to, Tonne, who was now holding a close and quiet conversation with Vicky at the other end of the bar. Electronic control in industry is not a subject for bar talk anyway, particularly with somebody who, I felt pretty sure, knew bugger-all about it. Demand and supply-side lags in hunting control mechanisms require a knowledge of integral calculus, rather than Covent Garden tits. I gave him a brief run-down.

'It's written for trainee engineers at student-apprentice level. People working for Higher National Certificate would want it, so would established instrumentation engineers going into control for the first time. I deal with practical problems – like stiction in contact galvos, surge suppression techniques in inductive relays, things that theoretically don't exist till you're stuck out in a field on a wet cold day trying to neutralize a flocculating tank.'

'That man can't read or write a word of English nor add two and two – you know why? His mother was Irish, his father was Irish.' Ragusson was talking about Tonne and telling an Irish joke at the same time. The girl was now, I felt certain, being talked to by the Belgian about me; he has his nose into her breast and his drink, from my angle; she was looking past his head towards me. 'His name is Danny and he owns this chi-chi wine bar,' Ragusson added. 'He does translations for me – Russian and German.'

I was not interested. I was thinking how could a girl like Sandra, tuned to every minute fragment of English suburban life, tuned to our holidays in Salcombe, Portreath, the New Forest, tuned to cups of tea in bed, how could she now be living with a bloody foreigner in Brussels?

'Tell me about your problem?'

Ragusson was looking into my soul, rudely. 'There is a woman,' he hazarded. Then, seemingly unconnected but connected in a metaphysical sense by his penetrating eyes, he said : 'What do you know about extra-sensory perception, Alec? May I call you Alec? My name is Mr Ragusson.'

'Nothing,' I said.

'Oh yes you do,' he said. 'When you were selling your electro-encephalograph in Gdansk – Danzig – ESP was the end product. Thought transference by brain-rhythm control and drugs. That is the book I want from you, Mr Ranger.'

'I know nothing about it,' I said.

He said : 'The book is already written. In Russian or German. It is the bible at the institute where you were working. I want you to go back to Gdansk and find it. I want the English language rights in that book.'

'I'm not interested. I didn't come to you for a job. I've got a job. I've got two jobs. I came to you to get my textbook published. What are you on about?'

He said : 'Have a brandy, Alec. I get on better with people if they are befuddled. How would you like to fuck Vicky?'

'From the front,' I said.

'Vicky!' he called. She came obediently, sniffing the air as if for dangerous gas. 'Alec is going to take you home,' he told her. I told him I hadn't got a car with me. 'In a taxi,' he said. Two minutes later we were out in the sunshine in King Street looking for a taxi, I and this stranger, now dressed in a warm trouser suit and wearing a little fur hat.

'Do you mind if I stop off at Sainsburys? I want some food for my dog.' I said I didn't mind. 'Have you got a dog?' she asked, searching for a link. We found that we've both got dogs, we both find it expensive feeding them now, we both live alone, neither of us mind travelling by tube when we can't find a taxi. I live at Chalk Farm, Vicky is the next stop on. I held her arm across the road and we stood and stared into the butcher's window as if it was a jeweller's.

'I don't know what to get him every day,' she said. 'He won't eat pet food. He doesn't know he's a pet. He thinks he's a people.' It really gave me the shivers to hear her say that. That's what Sandra used to say about Moosh. I told her to leave it to me and I bought a pound of rabbit and a pound of pigs' melts, chopped it up together after taking out the bones, then mixed it up with dog-biscuit meal. Bloody dog wouldn't touch it. 'It's that dog biscuit,' Vicky said. 'I meant to tell you.' Together we squatted on the floor of her bed-sitter and picked out the bits of dog biscuit with eyebrow tweezers. 'I feel I've got to know you already,' Vicky said.

The dog, a huge grey Great Dane, lay patiently watching us, with its arms folded. Everything we did in that room it watched us. And she said – sorry I'm not putting things in order – Vicky said, 'Are you a good friend of Laurel and Hardy's?'

This is what she and her colleagues and friends and clients at Danny's Cave call Ragusson and Geoffrey; the Viking big and fat and with a cold eye, his editor a little grey, tufted, apologetic cry-face. It is a very good description. I told Vicky about my relationships that first day. 'I wouldn't get mixed up with them,' she said. 'He'll get a hold on you. Ragbag gets a hold on everybody. Mr Neasden's been to prison. That's why he can't go anywhere else.'

'Geoffrey has? What the hell for?'

'Sexual offences,' Vicky said. 'He slept with his own daughter. That was after his wife got killed. His daughter's really beautiful. She works with me at the bar sometimes. Well, she got brain damage. She can't do a proper job now.' She was not aware that she had said anything funny or tragic or scandalous or disparaging about her own status or her place in the hard world. She said: 'I expect you'll meet Morag.'

And this gave me the shivers. If Sandra had a daughter she was to be called Morag. I've always liked the name Morag. It's got a kind of Gothic mystery and romance about it. Of course, I do realize there must be plenty of ugly stupid unromantic girls around called Morag.

'Mr Neasden was driving,' she said.

'What?'

You'll bear me out, if you're not interested in someone you're damn certainly not interested in what happens to them. I have told you about this first day of going out into the sunshine and smelling the last of the flowers and meeting someone after twenty years and meeting others and about the meaningless talk in the bar and ending up with this breasty nice doll in Belsize. And then remembering my own dog is waiting for walkies and to be fed and not staying for sex. 'I go to bed now and I have to be up again by five to open the bar at six,' Vicky said. 'Will you be coming back, Alec?'

'No,' I said.

It had been an interesting day, but the emphases were zero. Nothing that happened or had been said or implied gave me the slightest inclination to want to continue. It didn't seem to me that I'd ever see any of them again; the book MS would arrive back with regrets a few weeks later. You meet old friends, you catch up on a few old tragedies, they catch up on yours – goodbye. If you ever stop to wonder about what happened to so and so, don't bother; forget it.

Will you be coming back, Alec? No. It had been a nice day, the sun shone, I smelt the flowers again. Enough to know the hard world is still there, you don't have to visit. I could do without Covent Garden, wine bars, creepy old Geoff. Vicky was the nicest thing in the day; she proved that woman was still possible, though she would never be the same again. If Sandra was never coming home and if ever I was going to fall in love, a different sort of love again, it would not be with a Vicky. But she had restored some confidence in me. The smell in the morning was no lie, the chill wind on my skin, the breeze riffling the fine hairs on my scalp, the spring in my walk in November, caring about what I wore, putting on the style again, meeting the hard world again without getting the shivers.

Getting my face off the ground at last.

Putting on the style? I'd been home I don't know how long, a long time, I'd fed Moosh and slept off the drink and fried a meal and was considering a bath, a change into some new clothes and maybe spending the evening at Dingwall's Disco at Camden Lock before I realized I had left my shopping in Danny's Wine Bar. How did that happen?

'They're quite safe, Alec,' Vicky said when I telephoned her. 'I put them behind the bar.'

'What the hell made you put them behind the bar? That's why I forgot them!'

'Danny told me to. Mr Tonne.'

'Why? Doesn't he know they're mine?'

'I don't know. It was when you went to pee. You're not cross, are you? He did ask Ragusson, I think, and Mr Neasden.'

'Geoffrey knew they were mine!'

There was a short nothing, then she said, quite transparently evasive: 'Oh, I see. He must have forgot.'

'You're lying, Vicky. It's Laurel and Hardy doing their act, isn't it? They want me to go back. It's the master mind at work. What is he? Some kind of lunatic?'

First he gets a little hold and then he gets a big hold. First he finds out I don't drink then he finds out I had a problem and then he's looking for my weakness and soon he's using it. For what? Do you think Ragusson wants me to go to Danzig and bring back a hot book? It wasn't the way I saw it at all.

All I saw was a small publisher of textbooks trying to impress a new author with his big-time connections.

'I've got to go,' Vicky said then. 'I've got nothing on.'

'You won't last ten seconds on the Northern Line,' I told her. She laughed and I laughed and she said : 'Are you coming in tonight to pick up your things?'

I told her I wasn't. I'm an engineer, that's brighter than the average master-mind.

'You bring them in here on your way home tonight,' I told her. 'Then I'll run you home in my car. This is the address . . .'

Pretty soon I was going to have sex again.

2

I'm an engineer. I met Sandra in an almost empty Boeing 707 flying between New York and New Providence Island. That sounds high power, doesn't it? It's not, really. Writing it up now there's a temptation to swagger. You feel self-conscious you're not a private eye or special agent. Because in fact I was in America for my very first time, excited as hell, looking down all the time, every plane I rode in. The trip was paid for by a civil engineering contract and I was studying traffic signalling systems. This all comes under automatic control; wherever there's a supply and demand, wherever you can replace people with transistors, you send for me. And you know how the light stays at red whenever you're in a hurry? Me.

There's a very delicate thing I had to do now and that's describe this first meeting with Sandra McPherson; without saying anything that's been said before about a girl, I mean, or going on, or breaking down. I suppose for most people there is one bit of magic in the human experience that remains with them, bright as a jewel, for ever. They have to shine it occasionally, I expect. There's this opal hair slide that was in her hair that day which is in my Sandra museum at Chalk Farm, where we lived together for five years. When I look at it I can see her face pressed against the porthole, looking down as I was looking down through this immense sky on to the slowly changing face of America, the Delaware valley, Georgia, Carolina, Chesapeake Bay, all the little aeroplanes swimming below us like tropical fish and we two in a big empty Boeing. We shared the excitement at first with reserved smiles, the way we strangers do, and then with cigarettes and lighters and a

25

tray of drinks and chatty conversation. But somehow it seemed that we were meant to be there together and that we would probably fly on for a number of years.

Our conversation, as I remember it, went like this :

'I love you.'

'And I love you.'

'I love you, love you, love you.'

'I love you more.'

To be accurate, no such words were spoken. There was a twenty-two-year-old Scottish girl with straight brown hair, a perfect nose with an imperfect little bit extra at the end, her lips rather too thick, her eyes putting everything right and defying contradiction. There was a mind and a character, spirit, soul, heart, intentions good and bad, certainties and doubts and high ambition, modesty, style, daintiness, passion, integrity, sin and forgiveness and pain and positive thinking and all the other bits which I had missing and which could never be found anywhere else nor ever again.

'I love you.'

'I love you.'

'And I love you . . .'

And the Boeing came down to the turquoise islands and her husband was meeting her, for they preferred flying separately because of the children and it was not likely that we would ever meet again unless a miracle happened. And it happened.

Six months later the telephone rang in the sales office and Elaine Bowen answered it. 'It's for you – Sandra McPherson.' She exaggerated the Scottish accent.

'Is that Alec Ranger?' said the voice. 'You may not remember me, but . . .'

For the present, that's just about as well as I can do. That we became the single creature in a single shell, hold it to your ear, love I you love you I you love I I I I, on wheels, dog Moosh in the pouch, good dog love I you dog you I I I, see it sitting in Sunday queues, barricaded behind doors taking instructions from telly, can't come out, can't separate, woof woof woof, money money money, fuck love I me woof you hate go away – the evolved fortress, the couple, the lovers, the family unit, the unadventurous, secure, unchanging, boring, sterile, frightened to look, frightened to touch, frightened to feel, I love you and I love you and I love you and recurring, that we became the typical happy couple, in other words, was our disaster. Plus God and it would be a petrified stone horror.

Then there's just you and the dog, Moosh. Bark, doggie, someone's coming, is she coming back to us, our missing wall?

One o'clock in the morning, Vicky arrived. No parcels.

'Where are my new clothes?'

'What a lovely flat!'

They all say that, especially the women, for the fortress is built with a delicate tasteful touch. Alec in Sandraland.

'Is this her?' they say.

Sandra in a little flowered dress talking to a big white goose on the edge of Ullswater, Sandra in tight white trousers being Spanish under palm trees in Devon, Sandra in Portugal, in Scotland, on Skye, sailing at Salcombe, picnicking on the disused American wartime airfield at Great Gransden, Huntingdon, using the airfield perimeter road, shell-pocked, crumbling, now surrounded by corn and crops, to learn to drive on, 1970, 1971, 19 – always until we're both old people, living separate lives.

'Are these her clothes?' Vicky asked.

'Where are my parcels?'

'Mr Neasden took them back to his office.' She was browsing around the room, looking at the Sandra exhibits, the markings on the cell walls to mark all the days and nights of love, the drawings, the cardboard fish, the mobiles turning in the same draughts from the same barred windows.

'Back to his office?'

'He took them back to the office for safety – Oooh! Are these jewels real?'

Women know more about jewels than men do. Real women. This one question told me more about Vicky than her tits, for instance, did. This beautiful sexpot from the country who didn't know jet from amber was about seventeen and had never had either. I would think she's had everything else.

'Of course they're real.' Everything's real. All that junk that was so vitally important on a Sunday parole in places like Broadstairs (the jet) and Burnham-on-Crouch (Victorian tumbler) and which finally hung unused over the mirror, part of the prison furnishings. 'Why didn't she take them with her?'

'I hid them.'

'But they're hers.'

There was utter incomprehension in her blank pretty doll face. She had a short fur coat on hanging open and her nipples were pushing through the little pink silk uniform of Danny's Bar. I suddenly got something hard going that I hadn't had for a long time, not since Sandra made her flying visit back to collect her possessions. Cured or not now, a new man or old, I decided to give Vicky the full Sandraland tour – it includes a hundred and twenty colour snapshots and sixty minutes of her Scottie voice heard unaware after a day at the office. It includes all the oakum picking and mailbag sewing of the best jails – bits of embroidery, weaving, montages of rubbish, bottle-tops and the like, stuck on hardboard and sprayed silver; it includes candles made in jam jars and stains on the sheet.

'Do you still love her?'

That's all I need after doing the full course at two in the morning; that softly spoken question and a soft breast to cry on. This was the first time I heard Suffolk in Vicky's voice – the musical question. You might think, if there were no parcels to bring me, why did she call at all at this time of night, breaking her tube journey home, the last train. *You* might think that – but not I, Alec Ranger, engineer, lady-killer, broken-hearted and deserted. How irresistible.

'What ever made her leave you?' Vicky asked, after we had had sexual intercourse several prolonged times in Sandra's museum bed. She said (I promise you), 'I think you're lovely.'

The habits of the flesh are the lock and the key and the bars; their duration is the duration of the sentence. If we could get off the bed and go and do it to somebody else the relationship would stand a chance.

'Do you like this?' asked Vicky at four o'clock.

'Yes.'

She said, between oral caresses, 'I've only had two men since I came to London. One of those was John.'

'All right, let's try again.'

Ragusson sent her, of course. By the morning – I realized afterwards – this dumb, pretty, sexy cave girl knew all about my bereavement, where Sandra works in Brussels, about how she fell in love, was conned, betrayed me, whichever way you care to look at it; about Jacques Conte. By the morning Vicky knew more than you do at the moment. I was being set up. We are coming towards the beginning of the story.

'Ahem,' said Geoffrey Neasden.

This is a week later and I still haven't got my new clothes. Oh, all the excitement has gone. With me, even buying clothes is a sign of madness. I wear the same corduroy jacket for seven years. Well, we all do. Have a look round the instrument exhibition at Earls Court. We still dress like Marconi. This was one of the things that drove Sandra to escape. Then I go out and spend sixty pounds on denims, T-shirts, zip sweaters, waisted shirts to fit my emaciated state, blue and white hockey boots, start cultivating a bit of broken English; if she met me in the *strasse,* unprepared, she would flutter her eyelashes at me. So I planned a week ago. Now it's raining.

'I've got your things at home. Ahem. Your shopping. You left it in the wine bar.' I just stared at him and made him clear his lying throat three times. 'Morag thinks they're terrific. That's my daughter. Why don't you dress like this, dad! She wants to meet you. Ragusson's read your manuscript. We're going to do it.'

'Scotch or beer?'

'Oh. Ahem. Just the half. Ta.'

It's the same day of the week, the same time of day, the same pub, the Lamb, in Covent Garden. Soon Geoffrey is going to say it's a bit crowded and noisy, why don't we go to Danny's Wine Bar? You want to bet?

'Do you find it a bit noisy in here?'

'What? Eh? Hm? Do which?'

'Danny's...!'

Watch him as you walk behind him, little man in a brown suit, face full of money trouble; Laurel going to meet his Hardy. To upset the old routine, all you have to do is trip them up, surely. Or stick your fingers in their eyes. Or cut their tie off. What I did was hook my foot round the front of Geoffrey's ankle as he was going down the two stone steps out into King Street. He fell flat on his face on the pavement; he didn't even put out his hands to save himself. When I turned him over his nose and mouth were full of blood.

'Sorry! Ahem! Silly! ... Wine bar ...!'

The ant struggles to return to its hill. No chance, Geoffrey. Meet the new Alec Ranger; no prisons, mate. Let me give you a tip. You can recognize prisoners by the way they comb their hair, look at the clock, dust their little ornaments.

I'm nearly ready to kill the dog and eat it.

What's that hospital just off the north-east side of Trafalgar Square? There, anyway. We sat there in out-patients for half an hour before I started scratching. I refused to be infested. Women in November clothes, tramps tied up with bits of string, the odd stockbroker jerked off the production line by some minor mishap, some fat ugly black sister at the signing-in desk, young boy doctors snooting through, post-graduate heroes among the lepers. Germs and fleas jumping across the floor.

Geoffrey mumbled something about not bothering to wait, his words and throat clearings coming through lips now swollen as beef red sausages. He had no idea that I had done it deliberately and I felt quite sorry that I had. But I shall never again tolerate prison predictability in anyone.

'Who these tablets for, ma'am?' the black sister was asking a thin worried lady by the desk. 'They are for my husband.' The Bonga queen frowned a thick disapproving close-eyed look at the label. 'These are very strong tablet. You husband must come for these himself.' 'My husband is too ill. He is in pain. These are the tablets he always has.' 'If you collect them you

have a signed certificate from your doctor. I put them up here.'
'I must have them. He's waiting. The doctor doesn't open until tonight!'
'I put them up here. You get certificate or your husband come in.'
'My husband is dying, you silly black ape!'
A black doctor came into the doorway behind the desk; all of us casualties were getting interested.
'What de problem, Sister?'
'Get on the floor,' I told Geoffrey.
'Ahem – what?' he said.
I pulled him from the chair by his legs, got hold of his feet, ignored his kicking and struggling and exclamations, dragged him on his back across the floor. We took attention from the desk, the medical staff now stared at me.
'It's okay, I'm taking him home, he's dead now.'
They could see Geoffrey was not dead; the sister and the doctor came and knelt over him. 'He got run over,' I said. They got Geoffrey to his feet, took him into the surgery. I got the bottle of tablets from the shelf above the desk and gave them to the woman; she went without smiling, as if it were all part of the hospital routine. I stood outside the hospital and smoked until Geoffrey came out with his face painted bright red like a warrior. The new instant dressing.
'I telephoned Ragusson,' I lied. 'I promised to take you home.'
In case you've missed it, the object was to collect my shopping and not piss around Covent Garden for some obscure purpose of Ragusson's. 'What about my mack and my brief-case?'
I said: 'It's not going to rain and you're not going to do any work.' He said: 'I ought to just pop in.'
By which time I had a stationary taxi.

I hate Wembley. Street upon street upon road and avenue and crescent and close of semi-detached prisons. The rich I can stand and the poor are always with us but that red-brick status-conscious in-between land depresses me. Then there are

31

all those overblown associations with great events in the moron's calendar, FA finals, athletics, royal handshakes, the exhibition ruins. Just after the war it used to be on my road to Fuller's Earth where I did flocculation control. In my head there are all these little patches of England where I put in process control; and all these roads leading to them. To sewers, to dyeworks, flour mills, food factories, taking out men and putting in buttons.

'This is it. Ahem. Here we are, Alec.'

I know this house! Joyce lived here. We used to make love in the garage. But if she lived in Wembley why did she travel from Waterloo and why did we make love there? Because it wasn't Joyce at Waterloo, it was Mary Malting who ran the house journal at Weatherby's.

'It belonged to Joyce's parents,' Geoffrey said as he let us in, then calling into the house: 'Morag! It's only me! She'll wonder what I'm doing home at this time. Ahem.' I could see that he was getting nervous at having to explain himself to his daughter.

My God, the same hall stand (the one with a padded seat over the telephone directories), the same furniture; the working classes inherit mortgages and rubbish. I crept around this house as a lad of twenty or so, already married, already a father, already impregnating other girls. My time in prison was well earned, getting betrayed and deserted was overdue. However, not subscribing to any of the better-known world religions I feel mean about it. If you know that you are a good man, certainly a good engineer, which is all most gods claim, if you have no particular sins apart from carelessness, why accept retribution?

'Remember this?'

Geoffrey was pointing to a photograph in a family album. How many people keep family albums these days? It was a picture of two young men and an enormous motor-bike outside the Polytechnic in Northampton Street, Islington.

'Good lord. That's me and Kingston Blackie – good heavens, you were Kingston Blackie! I'd forgotten that. You were a real raver.' Geoffrey cleared his throat and laughed, modestly.

I'd quite forgotten his image, the black leathers and the bike and the girls and all the trouble with the law.

'You never came on that bike,' he said.

'I would now.'

'I wouldn't,' he said. And he said : 'There's Joyce – now do you remember her? She worked there.'

What a lovely girl. Good legs, she had; a dark, intense face, eyes always searching your face for the truth. Some women are like that. They're very vulnerable and deserve far more than they ever get. How strange that Geoffrey never knew about us. And then quite suddenly I was looking at Sandra. My Scottie Sandra, the loveliest eyes in the world, the straight hair, the long nose, thick lips, shyness, daintiness – well, I've done all that. But what was this picture doing in Geoffrey years before. 'That's Morag,' he said.

'That's Morag,' he said.

I asked him for a magnifying glass; the lovely face came up to fill the glass. It was Sandra.

'Nice, isn't she? Ahem. She wants to meet you.'

Something stopped me telling him.

'You'll find her a bit ahem odd. Since the accident. She had slight brain damage. She used to be brilliant. Now she's lost all interest. . . .'

I was not listening to him. By a freak accident my book finds a man who is the father of Sandra's double. I refuse to acknowledge that she could be in any way different.

'What sort of accent has she got?' I asked him.

'Who? Morag? Well it's funny you should say that. People think she's Scottish. She's never even been there? Isn't that strange?'

'No,' I said. 'Where is she?'

'Probably asleep. She sleeps a lot. Come and have a look – she won't mind. I'll get her to make some tea.'

Going up the stairs after Geoffrey, I made up my mind to marry Morag, sight unseen. Sandra had come back into my life. I have moods like this. It sounds ridiculous, doesn't it? I wouldn't write it down if I had anything else to do. We came to what is always the second-best back bedroom in a three-bedroom semi – the landing, lavatory and bathroom just as spacious as is necessary to turn round – and Geoffrey turned round before opening the door. There was a puzzled smile amidst the money in his grizzled eyebrows.

'How did you know that? About her accent? It was the strangest thing about her when she recovered. She was in a coma for a week. It was as if a different person came back to me.'

'That's strange,' I said. We were talking quietly at the bedroom door, not to disturb our subject. 'Exactly what date was the accident?' Incredible if it was the same moment that Sandra went to Brussels or fell in love with Jacques Conte or made love to him for the first time.

'January the thirteenth, 1965.'

It had no significance whatever; which seems even more incredible, doesn't it?

'Friday the thirteenth,' he added, as if reading a gravestone, 'I hit a lamp standard on the Watford Way. Joyce was killed instantly.'

'That's terrible, Geoffrey. That's really awful.' I always like to think people have died of old age; I had felt quite comfortable about Joyce being dead until now. Somebody must have told me about it but it hadn't sunk in. Yes, Vicky was on about it. 'You were driving, weren't you?'

'Yes. Ahem. I still don't know what happened, Alec. I shall never know now.'

'How absolutely rotten for you.' Along the Watford Way, too, was the feeling; it was like a novel written for the proletariat.

'I'll just see if she's awake,' he said, and tapped the door. You will notice that he had forgotten his question and I had avoided the answer. The big test was now; was I about to meet Sandra over again? 'Just a sec,' he said, and went into her bedroom. A black cat came out, rubbed itself against my legs and ran downstairs. Geoffrey appeared again in the doorway, inviting me in. 'That's a nuisance.' His face held much more than nuisance. 'She's not here and her bed's gone. I think she's gone again.'

It always takes me some time to work things like that out. Or rather, being an engineer, I work them out immediately but am not sure that I've got it right. I mean, how many daughters take their bed with them when they go out?

'What do you mean – shopping?' I said. It was clear to me now that Geoffrey Neasden had more problems in his life than I was aware of at our first reunion drink in the Lamb. I'm inclined to sum people up a little too quickly, just to dismiss them.

'No. God knows where she goes. This is why I was so interested in your trip to Poland, Alec.' I couldn't work that one out, quite; was he asking me to take Morag with me next time or suggesting that she was already leading a secret life with me? Things seem either vastly complicated or conspiratorial or else simple as rice pudding. And very often it depends on how you got out of bed. He alarmed me by sitting down suddenly where – at least that's what occurred to me – the bed used to be. Instead of falling backwards, however, he was sitting on top of a chromium pedestal ashtray and plinth, holding his damaged face with his hands. 'I'd like to get her electro-encephalographed,' he said, through his fingers.

'Oh, I see. Yes, of course. Good idea. Was it a single bed or double?'

Morag slept in a sleeping bag, it emerged; when she got the urge she simply rolled it up and put it on her back and hit the road, like so many of her generation. Where the bed had been there was a dust-free oblong on the brown lino in the corner of the room. It was a shabby, cold sort of room, full of useful clutter. There were clear signs to me that a prisoner had been incarcerated there for some years. Clutter starts like a doodle; if you know the signs you can trace it back to its origin and give it an approximate period. Morag's fulcrum of despair began with a toy sailing boat, waiting to blow her across the world, its keel lodged, in order to keep the sails upright, between two heavy volumes – *Zelda*, the story of the American writer Scott Fitzgerald's crazy wife, published in bound form about three years ago, and *The Once and Future King*, another huge book this one, by T. H. White. The cobwebs and dust of its stationary argosy anchored it to a framed picture of the actor Peter O'Toole, cut from a magazine and including the date of publication, 10 October 1972.

'She steals these books,' Geoffrey was explaining.

People who steal books rate one notch higher in my esteem than people who steal bread. I'm all for them.

'Of course. Ahem. I can't give her much pocket money. But then she won't work. She doesn't like housework. Her boy-friends have all got long hair. Window-cleaners and chaps like that. At fifteen she had seven O-levels, Alec. Literature, languages, maths, music – she still plays the tin whistle. Of course she cries a lot. Her mind is more sensitive than her knowledge. Her knowledge has all gone. She keeps coming up against brick walls. That's what she says. There's a great view from the window and she can't open the curtains. And I can't give her the clothes she wants. Or the drugs. She's on this and that. You know. This place stinks sometimes.'

Geoffrey got up and probed around the room. 'Her case has gone but I don't know what she's put in it.'

Lonely, shabby, heartbreaking room looking out on Wembley.

'A bit of bone penetrated the brain,' Geoffrey said. 'She went to sleep and she didn't quite wake up. That's what the doctor told her.'

'Is she depressed?' I asked him.

He thought about it, then smiled. 'No. She sings and plays the whistle. And fucks, I suppose. Sort of second-class now. I know that sounds snobbish. But if you knew the best things about Joyce – dignity, integrity, intelligence . . . Well, Joyce would be sad about Morag if she'd lived. I try to find both women in one sick child.'

'I lost my woman,' I told him. I had noticed that when little Laurel was talking from his heart he forgot to clear his throat. 'Yes, I know,' he said. 'Vicky was telling us.' He realized then that he had created a scene in my mind and cleared his throat. 'Well, she mentioned it. I'm sorry, Alec. You were together a long time, weren't you?'

I said: 'I don't think I was with anybody until I was with

36

Sandra.' Geoffrey looked up at me for a long time, then he said : 'I'll make you some tea then I'll get your things.'

What he meant by that was something quite different; people who think tea is just a drink are either fortunate, rich or imbecile.

Geoffrey needed a friend. He needed a friend more than his firm needed another textbook on process control. This is really why I was sitting in the living room of one-eighty-six Moribund Avenue, Wembley, Middlesex. Here is a man with a motherless child, a job he dislikes, put-upon, hard-up, no special talents, little initiative, too old to start again with a new company or in a new kind of job, there's retirement ahead and you know the filing system, then all at once an unsolicited manuscript is handed to him, sent in by a man he used to know.

'I always envied you, Alec,' he said, over the tea.

'But you were much more go-ahead than I was in those days. More daring, dashing – with-it, as we used to say. Clothes and so on, the Kingston Blackie image. Teddy-boy, almost.'

'I was fighting you,' he said. I did not understand him; specially at that distance. Then he said, as if breaking astonishing news : 'Joyce was in love with you, Alec.' I showed my incredulity to a nice degree and put it down with the lowered palms of both hands. 'It's true! All the time we were married you were her might-have-been. When she thought I'd failed her in some way she brought Alec Ranger up. Morag knows you. Ever since she was tiny. Your name, your picture, snippets of news about you. Like when you went to the States to study – what was it – anyway, I put that in three of our trade magazines with a photo.'

'I didn't know that.'

When Geoffrey laughed you could see Laurel crying and scratching his head at the same time. 'She might have had a better life with you. She would still be alive. Morag would be your daughter. I think you could cope with her, Alec.'

Only then did he clear his throat. I read him sufficiently well to know that this is what he hoped for. For the paragon to move in and do for Morag what he felt he should have let me do for her mother. This may sound like a lot of supposition.

'I wish she was here,' he said, several times. 'You must come again when she's here.' And he asked things like: 'Is there any chance of your girl-friend coming back from Brussels?' And: 'Are you now actually divorced, Alec?' Had I thought of marrying again and if so why hadn't I married Sandra. And how was my health. Last of all, what did I think of his boss, Ragusson.

'I think he wants people to think he's a gangster.'

'Ahem. That's not quite true, Alec. Ragusson *is* a gangster. One of the syndicate. You know.'

'He's not Italian.'

'Watch out, that's all,' Geoffrey Neasden warned me. 'Don't let him do you any favours, Alec. The repayments are too high.'

'What does Ragusson want from me besides my book?'

Geoffrey said: 'The Russians are into psycho-kinesis, whatever it is, mind over matter. Exploring unknown areas of the brain. I must say it interests me too. Because of Morag. There's a book written but not published yet. Not even behind the curtain. Ragusson wants to be the first Western publisher with a book on it.'

'The occult has never interested me,' I admitted.

'Not the occult, Alec. An applied science.'

There was something in his expression that betrayed passion and even hysteria. Not in the words. Then he said: 'My daughter can do rather remarkable things. Ahem. Since her brain damage. I'll get your things down.' He got up and went out quickly as if to stop questions.

As I heard his footsteps going up the stairs I had a most peculiar sensation of not being alone. This is not a B-picture horror story and I did not see the black cat; I just had a comfortable feeling of friendly company. Next moment Geoffrey was shouting down for me:

'Alec! Alec! Can you come up . . .' I went into the best bedroom, his own bedroom, where he had slept with Joyce. 'I'm afraid I've got bad news for you,' he said. He kept clearing his throat and seemed quite stupefied with embarrassment. I mean more than usual. When I went in he was walking backwards across the carpet looking up at the ceiling. 'That girl! Look at that! All over the ceiling!'

What she had done was stand on the bed and paint in several different colours – from a box of paints standing on the dressing table – a list of what appeared to be garments. It was headed: 'My Wardrobe' and included in columns:

2 prs knickers
1 petticoat
2 wearable dresses (jumble sale)
1 long skirt
1 mini skirt
2 prs tights
1 bloody bra
2 headscarves
1 teddy bear
1 woolly hat
2 tatty coats
1 wearable pair of shoes
1 pair of mother's slippers
1½ pair of earrings
1 jet necklace
1 set of silver sliver rings
odd and sods of beads
2 Premium Bonds

55 P
1 begging bowl
1 Morag
Mr Ranger's new clothes (super)
Thank you Mr Ranger
Goodbye dad
X X X X X X

Geoffrey had climbed on to the bed, his greasy Hush Puppy suèdes sinking into eiderdown and spring mattress up to his ankles; he reached up and touched scarlet paint on the word 'knickers'. His finger came away clean. 'Damn,' he said. 'That'll never come off.' There is something unchanging about the marital bedroom in the English semi; the suite itself which can never be arranged any other way, the wardrobe with its dusty top containing the only hat box she ever got, the green glass dressing-table set, the jewel jar full of safety pins, a couple of Doctor White's in the top left-hand drawer, long-haired rugs from Littlewoods' club, set of linen table mats, all the prison furniture arranged for eternity; and now, poor old Geoffrey seemed to be saying, this depressing list of his daughter's worldly possessions on the ceiling for ever, waking up on all the mornings of the rest of his lonely unshared prison sentence, 'I bloody bra'.

Geoffrey has got off the bed and is looking at me in abject apology. 'You know what she's done?'

'Yes,' I said.

'Morag has taken your shopping with her.'

'She's probably wearing it.' Judging by the list on the ceiling she needed it. Geoffrey thought for a second, then said :

'She wouldn't do that. Would she?'

'Why not?'

'They're men's clothes.'

This is when men like Geoffrey Neasden stand convicted. I used to be like that. Poor Sandra. Poor Morag. Poor any young woman stuck with people like us, the eternal prisoners. Soft people in a hard world; it gives you the shivers. They're men's clothes.

'What did they cost?' he asked, fearfully.

'Sixty pounds.'

'Oh my God,' he said.

I blew up the big coloured paper bags and burst them, one by one. She had left them on the carpet together with the bottoms of two pairs of expensive flared trousers which she had cropped off with – you might think – the bread knife. She was wearing my Confederate Army grey-green hat, my hockey boots, my Indian-embroidered chamois waistcoat, blue high-neck jumper with a yellow apple on the chest, yellow socks, green underpants, the whole super outfit. I could just see her with her sleeping bag on her back, her case, her 55p, hitching lifts on the motorways. To where?

'She's got friends in the country,' her father told me.

We were sitting in the living room again with more tea. This time Geoffrey had toasted crumpets. He didn't want me to leave. It was growing cold and dark outside in Wembley and he was going to be worried to death all night. I could see that his broken mouth and nose were hurting now, all the pink amyl-acetate peeling like sores from his lips and nose. I shifted the guilt on to Morag.

'She could have left you a note.'

He sniffed. 'Oh, I expect she has. One of her freaky letters. She does a lot of drawing and writing. Morag's very artistic. She makes things.'

'Does she make cardboard fishes?'

'Birds,' he said. 'That's one of her birds.' There was a cardboard bird covered in mauve cellophane hanging in the window on a bit of cotton. 'She won't go to work. That's why she hasn't got any friends, hasn't got any money, doesn't care how she dresses – I keep telling her.'

You could hear him; there was a nagging note in his voice. He realized it.

'Ahem. Well, I give her a pound a week pocket money. Clothes, cigarettes, pictures. No good giving her any more. She can't save. She can't save anything.'

The picture was dreary. You're young and pretty and full of urges, you've got a head problem and live in Wembley. Suddenly I could feel her in the room again, as if repaying me for the thought. There was no black cat this time but there was a skull looking at me from behind the sliding glass door of a bookcase. I went over for a closer inspection. A number of volumes had been removed to give it its own niche.

'That's one of Morag's friends,' Geoffrey said.

'What, from the country? He doesn't look very healthy.'

'Take it out. Go on, it won't bite you.'

I'd never actually held a skull before. 'Is it plastic?' It didn't feel plastic.

'Let's have a look,' he said.

I gave it to him and he put on some reading glasses.

'It's most probably Irwin,' he said. On closer examination of the jawbone, however, he said: 'No, it's Vincent.'

We both laughed again; he hasn't got much of a sense of humour. He said: 'I don't know where she gets them from. She's probably taken Irwin back. I expect it's one of these freaky things.' The name was scratched on the bone.

The phone rang. Geoffrey was in the doorway, agitated, hand covering the mouthpiece. 'I thought you spoke to Mr Ragusson for me?'

'His secretary,' I lied.

To the phone: 'He told Joan, Mr Ragusson! Didn't she tell you? Yes, he rang while they were dressing my face at the hospital — what? Oh yes, sir. I'll be in first thing — who? Oh. All right, I'll tell him. I hope I haven't put things behind this afternoon. Did Ralph get those drawings off to the block-makers? All right, I'll see to it — yes, I'll tell him. Thank you. Good night, Mr Ragusson. I'm very sorry — ' He got hung up on and came in, dejected.

'Oh, that's bad. You should have spoken to him personally. I thought you had.' He sat down, biting his fingers. 'Oh Christ, sitting here talking all the afternoon and him not knowing where I was. He sent Ralph all round Covent Garden looking for me. He wants you to have lunch with him tomorrow. Himself. Ahem.'

'I don't think I can do it.'

'What?' It was the very closest Geoffrey had come to scratching his Laurel forelock and crying his Laurel cry.

'I may have a heavy day tomorrow.'

'You still don't give a shit about anybody, do you?' Geoffrey Neasden said, enviously. 'Most of us have to grow out of that. Have some more tea then I'd better go to bed. I don't half feel rotten. . . .'

Oh yes, sir! Three bags full, sir. Who needs bosses? Poor old Geoffrey hasn't woken up yet. You haven't noticed me go to work yet, have you? I'll tell you when I do. It's little men who go home to little women and live in little prisons. Mon rebloody pose. I went home from Wembley on the tube to Finchley Road and found a taxi at Swiss Cottage to take me to Chalk Farm.

I've got a first-floor bay-windowed room in one of those white-washed Victorian villas you probably pass when you're ducking up through Belsize from the Round House to miss the traffic on Haverstock Hill. I hate the place now, to tell you the truth. Mentally I've left it. Every time I go in in the dark, even after twelve months, I find she's gone. Sandra, I mean. I committed suicide here one night.

Well, nearly. Nearly as I'll ever get. It was after the attempt to get her back had failed. After waking in fright that night, four weeks after she'd gone abroad to do a bit of temping, dreaming that her soul had fled from Chalk Farm and that she no longer loved me. I paced the floor all night not wanting to get her out of bed, half afraid to hear a man's voice. Yes, it was after that lonely ordeal and after that terrible early-morning telephone conversation with an angry stranger, hardly Scottish now.

'But I don't want you over here, Alec! I want to be alone a little while. I want to think. This is my place, I don't want you intruding. . . .'

Intruding? After five years when she'd run all the way home from the tube just to make sure nothing had changed. Yes yes, it was after that and after finding a neighbour to look after our child, Moosh, and after the panic flight to Brussels and after that terrible Saturday with charming Jacques Conte waiting to climb back in her bed and after the terrible lonely journey back on the Sunday with the whole world lost, one prisoner gone, the other in solitary.

'If you make out all right,' I told her in one of my two thousand letters, 'will you send for me and Moosh?'

In Westerns, the one that gets away brings the army back.

As an engineer, I planned to die. I planned to drink a whole bottle of scotch and swallow a whole bottle of sleeping tablets. What I did wrong was drink the scotch first. Halfway down the bottle I started tap-dancing. That was the first bottle; it was a bottle a day after that. I lost three stone in three months, grew a beard, wore rags; if Sandra had seen me then she would have fallen in love with me. Now my clothes fit and suit twenty-year old girls like Morag, chop three inches off the legs. If anyone wants me I'm the thin curator of the Sandra McPherson museum.

'Al'k! Al'k! Al'k!' That's Moosh talking while I'm unlocking the door. Poodles can't say Alec.

3

Years went by. In our engineers' language. Don't worry, you
haven't missed anything. Actually it was a few weeks, I suppose. Christmas coming up. I'd forgotten about Geoffrey
Neasden. And his mystical daughter. Whether she came back
I don't know. Ragusson, Tonne, Danny's Wine Bar, Vicky
whatever-her-name is, my book on process control, all gone;
that was last month. Geoffrey is probably still bleating at old
Ralph about subbing and Morag about her pocket money. In
this hard life if you haven't seen anybody for twenty years,
take it from me, you don't need them.

One has one's own little orbit. East Finchley night school
on a Wednesday evening, the stone corridors clacking with
platform soles, young men in high heels. Jeni Thirshall just
going in to take social philosophy. Hello, Alec. Hello, Jeni.
And then instead of going in with her class, which she usually
does after we've exhausted our repertoire, she had a double take
and stayed for a moment.

'Are you all right now, Alec? You look very well. What
have you done? I didn't recognize you at first. Thought you
were a student. I must say you look singularly resplendent
with that beard! One of my students asked me who you were
last week. Any news from . . . ?'

I shook my head, but not in despair. No, darling; I am
still available, are you? Her sympathetic smile had a hint of
congratulation in it, coupled with a tiny, excited fear. My
confidence is insufferable now, I might add. The last time we'd
been alone together I was crying in her lap. Jeni Thirshall is

45

yacht country; the slender middle-class English rose with an honours degree whom you know to be untouchable without a ring or a promise. In Jeni's case you had to be a barrister, preferably with a boat at Lymington. I was lucky enough to catch her on the rebound from one of these once, long ago, soon after I'd started teaching; it was a glimpse of Shangri La never seen again. Not yet. When a woman lowers her defences in a weak moment and then puts them up again you are fighting a double battle from then on. One of the battles is with what she thinks you now think of her. It is too late for her to pretend she doesn't do it, so she doesn't do it. You really need a slide rule with women.

'You dirty sod!'

This is not Jeni talking. This is David Ballantine who has come up behind me while I am still making plans about Jeni who is now on her way to her desk inside the classroom.

'And this time,' David said, 'you're going to open the door.' He held both my shoulders and looked at me as if I was a newspaper. 'You're over it!'

'I'm not,' I said, stubbornly.

'Don't look broken-hearted now. It's too late. Where's that miserable, boring, deserted lover on the brink of suicide if you don't buy him another drink?'

I said : 'You know you can't come in, David? Three attendances in the whole term. You've been struck off the class.'

'Balls,' he said, cheerfully.

He came into class with me, sat at the front, grinning; didn't make a single note in an hour and half. He was a door-to-door salesman when I first knew him. When he enrolled for my classes on instrumentation he believed the course was about the inner workings of vaccuum cleaners, washing machines, toasters, television, radio, record players, tape recorders – all the things he was flogging. He thought he would get one-up on the average tally boy. He dropped out when he discovered that he was in the world of industrial measurement, but in the few weeks he attended my classes a strange thing had happened between us. I could see by his face tonight that if I became the least bit unwary another strange thing might happen. Certainly he had not come to listen to me talking about the null indicator in the automated Wheatstone Bridge circuit.

A null indicator, in case you don't know and I'm sure you do, is not Arnold, sitting at the back and looking vacant, but a coil of wire suspended delicately between two electro-magnetic poles which will deflect from its zero position with the passage of a minute electric current in one direction or the other. This deflection is used to move a pointer on a calibrated scale, or a mirrored light on a long ground-glass calibrated scale, or to activate a recording or controlling circuit which may (a) produce an ink graph or (b) cancel out the change which gave rise to the departure from zero – i.e. by moving a flow valve to control a chemical process. The first question David ever asked me, after sitting silent and blank for three weeks of this kind of thing, was :

'Is that your old American car outside, Mr Ranger?'

The answer to this question, which was 'Yes', nearly put me in prison and then led to this strange thing we have between us – friendship. We know the best and the worst about each other and when Sandra went he probably saved my life or my sanity. For a time I hated him and avoided him because he competed with my memories of her; because I had not channelled every last ounce of love into her. My miserable conscience in bereavement said I should not have needed another friend. David knew this and played it cool and watch-ful and now, I would say, we were out the other side. Me without Sandra, David with a problem marriage. The recorded history of the world, they say, is only dust-thick on the planet. We've known each other ten years longer than we've known our women.

'Mr Ranger, sir!' David was putting his hand up. 'I like your new beard, sir.' This brought a laugh from the class, eighteen male, four female; he could never stop being Tommy Cooper or Chick Murray or some other comedian. Come to think of it, Oliver Hardy he does very well. I shaped a kiss to him and got another laugh. You can be camp without fear when you're as ugly as I am. David is big, ginger and twenty years younger.

While they copied the circuit from the board and made notes I sent a note to social philosophy, using Elaine Bowen – from our sales office, you may remember – as a messenger. Bit unfair, really; Elaine would come to my classes if I taught Theban. 'Jeni – will you have a drink with me tonight? Alec.' Elaine came back with the reply and a satirical light in her eye while I was demonstrating the ticker mechanism in my lab recorder to David.

'Not tonight,' Elaine said. 'Another night.'

'Couldn't she write it down?'

David said : '*I* want you tonight. That's why I'm here. I've written a play about you.'

'I didn't know you were a playwright?' Elaine told him.

David Ballantine is David Ballantine. A bit of everything.

David's mother, Molly, was a Tiller Girl, for any of you old enough to remember what that was. She is now a clairvoyant old-age pensioner. She makes uncanny predictions about people and sometimes smells the future. She smelt chemists' shops the night before David found his father dead in one, of a heart attack. She always knew David was going to be successful but she didn't know what at.

'Keep sniffing, Ma,' he told her, every time he loused up another career. He never had jobs, they were always planned operations. When we met he had three projects, as he called them. One was raising funds for a football team or a club or whatever it is. I found out more about lotteries than I ever knew before. Did you know they keep the winning tickets in their pockets until they've sold enough to cover the prizes?

'The printers do that automatically,' he told me.

'But you don't know the winning numbers until they've been drawn.'

'Oh, come on !'

This time he was giving away a new car and the draw was taking place in the middle of the football field just before a special benefit match. David first of all tried to find a celebrity to take the ping-pong balls out of the drum and call out the wrong number, but decided that was too risky. Then he hit on the idea of bringing a famous strip cartoon character to life, preferably somebody in a mask to confuse the evidence in court if anything went wrong.

'Superman?' I suggested.

'Batman and Robin,' he said. 'That's why I want your car. I'll pay you for it.'

'It's not a Batmobile.'

'I'll dress it up.'

I said : 'Who's playing Batman?'

He said : 'I don't know yet.'

'Who's getting the new car?'

David didn't know that, either; he could never find anybody with enough imagination to go along with his schemes. I pointed out the risks. Whoever drew the winning ball would drop it, it would be windy, the mayor would pick it up.

'I'm putting the mayor in the stadium and not allowing any policemen on the field,' David said.

In the event everything went terribly wrong. The mayor would not stay in the stadium, the police went on the field, there was no chance of calling out a wrong number and in fact, fact being what it is, the number drawn was one David had previously arranged to be drawn with a friend who had refused to participate in the swindle. David went round to his house that evening of the match to claim a half-share in the new car. All he got was a glass of sherry. Well, not quite all.

'It's given me a brilliant idea, Alec − it was your car that did it. We went through the town before the match, Batman standing up waving − you should have seen the crowds! Not just kids. I'm going to get a concession on that character. Thousand pounds a week, that's what I'll earn. Opening fêtes, showrooms, advertising this and that. Two hundred pounds a day, just like that!'

It was the beginning of David Ballantine Promotions − 'We Bring Fiction To Life!' He brought Batman to life, he brought to life FAB 1, the pink, fully automated (with rear-viewing closed-circuit television) Rolls-Royce from the *Thunderbirds* television series − complete with chauffeur Parker and Lady Penelope.

'Alec, I want you to meet Lady Penelope,' he said one day in the Barge at Camden Lock. 'Penelope – this is Alec Ranger. One of my electronics men. By the way, Alec, I've got another job for you – what do you know about spacecraft?'

Three months later he went on the road with a full-scale reproduction of Apollo 8, the first American moon capsule. Mounted on a trailer, it tilted, tipped, galaxies moved past the portholes, tape-recorded messages authentically taken from the original space journey came from loudspeakers, astronauts calling base. Lady Penelope was now a space girl wearing David's idea of an irresistible space suit. 'See, it's got zips at the front,' he said. I found them one Whit Monday on Hartham Common fête by the river at Hertford, the whole circus. We had tea sitting at an iron table in the marquee, crowded with hot people, ankle-deep in beer bottles and ice-cream cartons.

'This is Sandra McPherson,' I said.

She wore a little white dress that day and had her hair in bunches.

'What kind of play?' I asked David later that night.

'Tea or coffee, Alec? Tea. Tea tea tea,' said Caroline.

Lady Penelope was no longer a space girl, she was Mrs Ballantine and had a part-time job with an estate agent. When she'd gone to the kitchen, David said:

'It's about us. Well, about you, really. When you came back from Brussels. I think I've sold it to *Love Story*. He gave me some clipped pages of typescript. 'Don't show it to Caroline. eh. . . .'

I wouldn't show it to anybody, not the way he had put it together. But I want you to read it now because it's part of the equation. Odd to get somebody else's view of that black day in the history of the world when nothing rhymed.

Half A Couple was the title. 'A television play outline by David W. Ballantine.' It was routed in red ink to Nick Parker, an ATV producer David had made it his business to meet during his *Thunderbirds* days; he had had some kind of publicity collaboration and had milked it for every contact he could make.

As a work of fiction, *Half a Couple* is about as creative as a railway line. Having got himself a producer, David had looked around at his friends, clapped his hands and said, now who can I sell? The recent harrowing melodrama to which I had subjected all my friends and relations was neat and ready-made. He had not even bothered to change the names. You will discover the problem, already mentioned, in his marriage to Caroline, you will get introduced to Sandra's best friend, Janet, also from Altnacealgah-by-Lairg, you may tune in to some of the big things followed by the little things (the kick up the arse, the bang on the head) mentioned at the beginning of this engineering report.

Certainly you will not receive the appalling shock that I received when I discovered that the one climactic bit of the story which I imagined he had put in to give it some kind of dramatic shape was in fact – fact. That at one stage Sandra had come back to me and nobody had told me. Friends think they know what's best for you but they don't. People are inclined to think that what happened between me and Sandra had happened before and would happen again. Not true. When I cry about Sandra it is for those unique patches of sunlight clear to the naked eye for the first time, the tidal pool remaining on the rocks at Portreath will do for now. A million tides will leave the same pool, for ever.

'Don't rush it,' David said. 'It's quite a complicated bit of writing. What it does is throw up images in the director's mind. See it like it's on a screen – know what I mean, baby?' I told him to shut up; messy and convoluted, here is what he wrote:

The play opens in the home of David and Caroline who no longer have sexual intercourse. She is bitter because of it, lets everybody know about it. He loves her but is helpless to put it right. 'If you had a twin sister I would bang the daylights out of her. To put it another way, you're perfect, but the excitement has gone. . . .' We don't get this situation immediately, just the taste of it. She is nearly naked and he is striking matches on her, as they say.

51

The telephone rings in this first scene, coming from under titles.

DAVID (to telephone) : Oh shit. I told Alec not to go to Brussels. Everybody told him not to bloody well go. Of course she's got somebody else –

('Lucky her!' Caroline puts in.)

Who's meeting him at the airport? Where's his dog? Are you leaving now, Janet? Look after him till I get there – I'll collect Moosh on the way....

This is how we learn that Alec is back from Brussels and Sandra is not with him. Sandra has found herself a Belgian. She is one of those Scots with colonizing tendencies, happy anywhere but Scotland, who confuses a foreign accent with ancient culture. She would warm to strangers who mistook her modified Caledonian accent for something Continental.

(These character touches of David's were so accurate that I began to get interested.)

In the early minutes of the play we see a rescue mounted by Alec's friends – David, a brilliant ideas man and entrepreneur, Alec's son Raymond, and Janet, Sandra's best friend, who has always been secretly in love with Alec and intends to cash in on his despair.

Late that night at Alec's Chalk Farm flat they try to comfort him. Also with him is Detective Superintendent Cyril Dyball who took pity on Alec on the flight from Brussels; by a coincidence he was also with him on the flight over. The policeman is married to a Belgian girl and assures Alec that Sandra will not for long tolerate the Flemish chauvinist male. This is a great scene and it becomes a kind of survival club for Alec. It is Janet who stays the night with him, however – end of first scene . . .
FADE OUT FOR COMMERCIAL BREAK.

Speaking as an engineer and as David's leading character in this drama I would like to take this unusual opportunity to comment before it goes into production. After Raymond, David and Cyril had gone, there was more drama that night than I ever disclosed. I'll give you diagrams of Cyril later in the text, for he's quite an important part and lubricates the murderous business in Brussels that follows; for now let us stay with the night I raped Sandra's best friend. It was quite unintended and Janet's own fault – or design – and not something either of us was likely to gossip about, once I'd persuaded her not to go straight to Camden Town police station.

Difficult for me to tell you what kind of state I was in that night; try to imagine a multi-vibrator circuit with all its volts missing. I was a baby who had lost its mother and its home and whoever was around was useless. Through everything they said to comfort, through a bottle of whisky, I could see Sandra on the plafform of that hideous underground station in Brussels, refusing to come close to the open door of the train where I was standing. I wanted to kiss her, I wanted to hold her, I wanted the familiar feel and smell of her to reassure me that she was not dashing straight back to the Avenue Molière to welcome her Belgian author. The door was about to shut.

'Please! Sandra! Let me kiss you!'

'No! You'll pull me on the train!'

So she knew what state I was in; what she was doing to me. I had slept all night on the floor of her bedroom, holding her foot; she made me a bed up in the next room and I had crept back while she slept. We slept together for five years, you understand, here in this room. Now suddenly, because of this Flemish stranger, I was not allowed to see her undressed.

'Don't fret y'sel, Alec! Och, it's just a passing thing!' Janet kept telling me. 'I know Sandra. You're the only man she's ever stayed with. She just flings herself in at the deep end and then swims to save her life. Look at that Yank and him wi' two kids! She hates kids.'

I met those two terrible American monsters just briefly when I was making polite chat with Sandra's husband who had come to meet her off the plane at Nassau airport.

'Hey, Parp! When we gonna eat?' Sandra trying to coax them into the car. 'Aw scram, Scottie! You ain't my ma! Hey, Parp! When we gonna eat?' Sandra fluttering an SOS at me with her eyelashes as they drove away. I could see her fluttering the same desperate signal to Jacques Conte when she had failed to stop me flying, knew that I was on my way to Belgium to bring her home.

'That's not true,' Janet told me, as part of her comforting.

'Look how she found you after the divorce. Two years later. Three thousand miles away. After one chat in a noisy plane. She loves you, Alec.' I had given Sandra an article of mine, 'Automatic Temperature Compensation in pH Measurement', torn from *Instrumentation*. At the time it was done to impress a lovely stranger as swiftly as possible. Back in London two years later she had used it to trace me through the journal. 'We met on a Yellow Bird flight to the Bahamas in 1967 – you probably don't remember. . . .'

Now bear in mind Sandra's Scottish appetite for exotic places and exotic men while I make a confession. One of the other things I did to impress her was convey the impression that I spent most of my life in Boeings, flying high above the humdrum. One of the New Men of science. I didn't mention traffic signals in Dayton, Ohio. About the shell of love, about the prison and the five-year sentence at Chalk Farm, I said nothing. I let her find out for herself.

'Let me ring her,' Janet said, at three in the morning.

'No!'

'Let me ring her, Alec! I'm her friend. We've known each other all our lives. I won't tell her I'm here.'

'You'll wake them up. They'll fuck each other again!'

'You're wrong, Alec. We're not like that. We don't jump out of one bed into another. Especially Sandra. If you can spend two years at Strathclyde and still be a virgin. Let me talk to her, Alec. Let me tell her what you're going through.'

'If you tell her I've just cut my throat she won't come back. Bloody fucking stubborn two-timing Scottish cow. She knew she was going to Brussels to fuck somebody. She as good as told me only I was so bloody certain of her I wasn't listening – I'll kill him! Bloody foreign twit!'

I had drifted into a sleep of emotional exhaustion, still dressed, lying on the rug, and I heard, as you do sometimes in sleep, noises about a hundred miles away which became Janet talking on the telephone, quietly, at the far end of the room.

'Janet?'

I had spoken before realizing she was on the phone. You know the size of these partitioned open-plan Victorian flatlets.

Apart from a tiny kitchen and tiny bathroom it's all you've got.

'Oh, just a wee minute, Alec – I'm checking the time.'

Having said such a stupid thing in the panic of the moment, she was forced to hang up on Brussels. Only an idiot talks to a recorded voice. Coming back across the room she said, casual as a death sentence, 'Three-twenty-five and forty seconds.' I looked up at my electronic, Greenwich-controlled mantelpiece clock and saw that it was five to four. So did she. 'At least, I thought that's what he said!'

'They've got a man on TIM tonight?'

'How do you feel now you've had a sleep, Alec?' she said. And she said things like she ought to be going and would I like some more tea and was I hungry. I pulled her down on the rug by her dress and put my hands round her throat. 'He was there, wasn't he?' I said. She said hardly anything else throughout the next half an hour apart from warning me that she would go to the police as soon as she left.

'This is what she's doing now!' I said, several hundred times.

It was not easy. You don't get erections in the midst of emotional agonies. If you analyse it I was doing something I'd promised myself ever since Sandra introduced us and making the excuse of substitution and anger. I kept calling her Sandra. The only way I could get my soft, sentimental penis inside her was by forcing her knees up and spooning it in.

'I hope you know what you've done, Alec Ranger,' she said afterwards. 'You've raped me. You'll go to prison now.'

I said: 'Let's go to bed, Janet. Make it worth while.'

She wouldn't do it any more that night but we slept together and she was kind again by the morning and willing to drop charges.

'What do you think of it?' David asked me.

They live somewhere like Tottenham over a dentist. You have to tiptoe around and shut doors quietly. Caroline had crept back with the tea and they were watching me read the play. 'He won't let me look at it,' Caroline said. She was small dark, petite, like every girl I'd ever seen him with. She was bitter on a long diet of pie in the sky. She said : 'I suppose it's about a couple who don't co-habit.'

'Sssh,' David said, 'eh.'

'Sssssh, he says. I used to be Lady Penelope.'

This was not a comic thing with Caroline. In her not too affluent life – there was a reasonable sort of first marriage with holidays abroad and a nice house in Epping – the period on David's promotions shone in her memory : hotels, crowds cheering her past, kids on the way to the moon. To a professional model it would have been just another job, but for Caroline it seemed that David had made her a queen and quickly demoted her. Very much the same kind of feeling between Sandra and me sometimes. We'd both met when we were in the air, flying high. Nine till six in a Tottenham Court Road office is not the same.

The second act of David's play *Half a Couple* – of which what I was reading was only a condensed synopsis, you understand – was about Alec's obsessive loneliness and misery and the attempts of his friends to stop him doing what is known as something silly. I never have understood this understatement. They were topping each other in this scene and that (DAVID'S FLAT : DAY) on the subject of their own special insight into Sandra's thoughts and feelings.

'If you want her to come back to you,' says Caroline, 'you must change everything she disliked. I mean, she stopped grumbling years ago, but it was all still there, simmering.'

I don't intend to list these things at present, irritating coefficients of the main factors (get divorce through at last without children finding out, buy farm in country, cottage in the Algarve, etc.) but the point is they all ignored the possibility that Sandra might be in love with Jacques Conte and feel about me the way I feel about Mary and Barbara and *ad infinitum* – a friendly connected kind of affection. She sent me a Christmas card (last Christmas) and a birthday card with no kisses on them, just 'love, Sandra', and no little dog's head with balloonage coming out to show to Moosh, or little girl diagrams of her latest bra.

56

If you're now getting me mixed up with *Half a Couple* you're dead right; I don't think David left anything out. Even what I thought he'd invented, as I have already mentioned, turned out to be true. 'You're not an individual any more,' somebody says in the play about marriage and shacking up and joining together like cells in amoeba; 'you're half a couple.'

This poor deprived, homeless semi-person, then, with all his habits cut off, slinks into the saloon bar of the Barge at Camden Lock, pulls out the same two stools and orders the same drinks – scotch and dry and brandy and Babycham. Drinks them both himself, alternating sips, hearing in his poor deranged mind (VOICES OVER SCENE) her Scottie voice chattering on about her day. Play it again, Alec.

'The gurrals get wurras and wurras. Maureen came into my office today, if you please. Would I do herer duplicating. I've shown herer how to use that blasted machine a million times. I furraget! she says. I furraget, Sandra!'

Put your drink on the ledge by the window and you can see the bus stop and the tube-station entrance. Watch for the little woollen head separating out from the next flock, the neat little smock-coat, serious, cold, boyish expression until she sees me waving and waves back. If she can, that is, depending on what she's carrying, what she's bought at lunch-time. As an engineer and curator of the Sandra McPherson museum, it worries me that I can no longer remember a handbag. I have an idea she rebelled against anything feminine; anything that gave any kind of support to the notion that a woman is supposed to do (or wear) this or that.

'Hulloo!' The little musical, two-note greeting on a descending third of the scale, whether for the telephone or submitting to your kiss. Same when she went out before me in the mornings, a little two-note whistle as she clattered by the window, no matter who was around. If she didn't I would worry all day. 'You didn't whistle this morning!' 'I did! I thought I did. Oh no, I saw the postman. . . .' I can play her little whistle to perfection on my flageolet and make the dog look up. I've got her flageolet.

'Good evening, Mr Ranger.' The six o'clock regulars come in. The nice chap who has some kind of nervous twitch and turns his head on one side to speak, his eyelids fluttering as if connected to his mouth. 'How's that little doggie, then? All right? Good, good.' You can't say anything to him except about dogs. The next chap you have to stick to your car or he'll think you are somebody else. 'Running all right, now? Lovely. Keep it wrapped up. Ice last night!'

'Excuse me – are you using this stool?' That's a pretty girl taking Sandra's stool and then you're half a couple. 'Had a good day?' he's asking her. There are no good days and no bad days when you're half a couple. Nobody cares.

And your eyes flooding again, seeing her reflection in the Double Diamond ad.

One night the miracle happened and the little woollen head left the group from the tube and came towards the pub, saw me staring, gave a little wave, came in; it was Janet. The obsessed see and hear what they want to see and hear. The same Scottie voice. Speaking as a trained engineer I believe Janet worked at it.

'You look awful, Alec! Are you all right?'

'I thought you were Sandra!'

'I'm sorry.'

'Will you have a drink?'

'I will. Brandy and Babycham. Is that okay?' What else indeed; and when it came, her eyelids fluttering her appreciation above the rim of the glass: 'Purrafect!' It was the first time – or maybe the second or third – I'd seen Janet since I raped her. We moved in different orbits with different friends. Sandra would sometimes join them when she broke out of jail; drink with Janet and Eileen, Lee and Ruth at Swiss Cottage. Come home sick.

'She's been back, Alec.' Who's been back? 'Sandra. I've been shopping with her. She rang me up. She was staying with Isobel in Wimbledon.' Sandra has got a sister Isobel in Wimbledon. I know her and I know Sandra's family at Lairg, mother, father with a heart condition, brother Donald and

Wee Jim, her sister's little boy – she's got these sis.
once Sandra had gone behind the barrier of silence I
bear to talk or correspond with anybody who might still
contact with her. Any casual information about a part of y
own body, heart, spleen, brain, genitals, is not on.

'Was she alone?' I asked her.

'She was alone when I saw her.'

'You know what I mean. Was she over here alone? Has she
got her Belgian author with her. Jacques the haque.'

'I honestly don't know, Alec. She didn't talk about personal
affairs. I don't think she's happy.' She saw me brighten and
went on : 'Nobody thinks she's happy. We had an evening with
the crowd. She wants some of her things. I said I'd collect
them for her, post them on. That's why I came here tonight.
Can I come back with you?'

All rubbish but I bought it. Of course they talked about
personal affairs. They've been chatting like machine-guns about
nothing else ever since the playground. Could you imagine two
Scottie lassies getting together for a wee dram after months
apart – one of them now shacked up with a foreign novelist –
and being at all reserved?

'He's really desperate, Sandra.'

'Och, he'll get over it! Alec'll soon find a birrud!'

What I wanted to hear was that Sandra had caught
venereal disease from her Flem and was pregnant by him and
had nobody to turn to but me. Apparently this was not so
far the case, or if it was she had not mentioned it to her old
friend. Later, too late, I revised their dialogue in my head. I
decided it was Sandra who was desperate to know that I still
loved her and Janet who painted a gay fresco of happy Alec
to keep her away.

'I've got a new flat,' Janet told me later that same evening
as we packed some things of Sandra's into a tartan case she'd
left under the bed. 'Trouble is, it won't be ready for two weeks
– they're decorating. I've got to leave my place on Friday.
Ruth says I can sleep on her floor but I don't fancy that.'

The suggestion to solve her accommodation problem, when
it came, appeared to come from me; women being what they

re. You will understand that I had not yet been sexually liberated. The world had not begun to rhyme yet, nor the breeze chill my face or riffle my hair, nor the chrysanthemums reach their tender souls into my nostrils. In short, I was not yet alive and anything I did with Janet was substitution therapy. And we did it quite a lot during the months – as it turned out – that we lived together in my museum. We did it up until a day when I was emptying the dustbin in the trash area at the side of the house and Janet's contraceptive pill container fell on the ground with Wednesday's safety and Friday's safety not used.

I now have to make an important statement about the women I have been telling you about. About Sandra, about Morag, about Vicky, about Janet, about Caroline, about Mary, about Barbara – now running a gift shop in the Bahamas (I was visiting her when I met Sandra) and about Joyce, now dead. The statement is this; I loved them all in different ways and they were lovable in different ways and I never had intercourse or an affair with a woman who was not a compatible friend at least; at least. Some men make love to strangers and so do women. I had a few drinks before writing this paragraph about women. As an engineer, which I am, twenty-four hours a day, into electronics and automatic processes, as, therefore, a rather precise and accurate man, I wanted to rough it up a little and try to get a degree of honesty beyond a neat phrase or two. I wanted you to thoroughly understand that Sandra McPherson is, much more than probably, the world's only perfect woman. I realize that I was incredibly lucky to meet her, incredibly fortunate to live with her for five years, from 1967 to 1972. I once met a young couple from Glasgow, old friends of hers, who knew her in her teens, and – it was in a big country house in Surrey and I don't remember what we were all doing there – the man took me aside during the course of the evening, drew me into a vast empty kitchen with an earnest look on his face.

'Alec. Listen. Listen. You've got a great girral there! Turrific!'

He then took me back to join the company.

The point is this: listen. Sandra would never do anything as devious as forgetting to take her pill. It is from the foothills that you measure the mountains. Jacques Conte, no matter how intelligent, how artistic, how human, how truly wonderful (which Sandra kept telling me he was) he is, cannot – cannot! – simply because he is a foreigner, know what he's got in Sandra McPherson. Something as dainty and perfect as a field daisy, something as sweet as a child's song, but with such roots of steadfast Scottish integrity as would hold up the Empire State Building. When God is doubtful about letting me in and asks for references, I shall say:

'Sandra McPherson loved me!'

Sandra McPherson is perfect, but she did not realize that I knew it. She did not know that I had sufficient quality to deserve her. She related me to my past history and she failed to see it, not being an engineer herself, as nothing else but the path I had trodden to find her. Any other man who has suffered less, or given less suffering, in order to qualify for her love, will, in the long run, fail her. A unique woman of her immense stature needs the hardened, toughened, tempered article to sustain her love, faith, fulfilment from here on to the grave. And enough shortcomings and weaknesses and vanities and infidelities to feed her fine outrage.

David's play ends then, on what I thought to be a fictional note.

ALEC'S FLAT: NIGHT Sandra opens Alec's room with her own key. The place is empty of people but the dog is excited to see her and she cuddles him. Mummy's come home. She looks round the old place, sadly. It is a museum to their life together but there are some new exhibits – Janet's. Sandra switches on the record player and an old favourite starts in the middle (Tell her Smokey Joe/was here and had to go). There is little indication that Alec has taken a new padwife since he still has Sandra's picture pinned up everywhere; holiday snaps, hotel bills. We see now that Sandra has a case outside which she brings in before telephoning and we cut to David Ballantine's flat – Alec and Janet are there. David takes the call in the hall.

'Who?'

'Sandra. I'm at home. Alec's place. Is Alec there, David?' Er, ahem, yes and no – what? 'I don't want to talk to him on the phone. Tell him I'm here and I'm waiting for him . . .'

'Who was that?' Caroline wants to know. 'Wrong number,' says David. From here on the scene is loaded. The news of Sandra's return is too big to give Alec. Instead David turns the conversation into a probe about the status quo – does Alec still want Sandra back and would it be fair on Janet who now seems solidly related. Not so :

Alec says : 'Of course I want her back. Janet knows that. I write to her every week. She knows it's still her home, still her dog.'

Caroline says : 'That's not very fair on Janet.'

Janet says : 'I love them both. If Sandra came back I'd go – happily.'

'She'll never come back now,' Alec says.

David plays God and invites them to stay for dinner.

Meanwhile at Alec's flat Sandra has discovered Janet's belongings in the wardrobe, the bedroom – the bed. She says a sad goodbye to Moosh and leaves. FADE OUT

'I don't like the ending,' I told David. 'Very unlikely. Sandra wouldn't come back and if she did you would tell me – instantly I should think.'

David and Caroline looked at each other and suddenly there were prickles in the air; I knew before they said it.

David said : 'But she did come back, Alec. And I didn't tell you.' He took the manuscript from me. 'This is just how it was – it was that night last August when you stayed to dinner.'

'For God's sake !'

Caroline said : 'Janet thought she was pregnant. She told me when you two were down the road getting a drink.'

'She wanted to be pregnant. She was skipping her pill. Do you mean Sandra came back to my place with her things? All the way from Brussels?'

It wasn't quite like that. David had made inquiries later. He had talked to Isobel in Wimbledon. She never moved out of Wimbledon. She was a skinny – well, I suppose she still is – attractive woman, older than Sandra, who had always been a nanny to rich families and finally had married into one. We had dinner with her sometimes and I quite fancied her, though she was inclined to be full of herself and her social engagements and she didn't appear to know anybody who was not a doctor or barrister or – oddly enough – a nun. She works voluntarily at a Catholic hospital. 'Sister Therese chased Sister Mary down the corridor with a hot sausage! It was so funny!' I used to wonder if she ever put her mind on being fucked, or just went on talking about the Lord Mayor's Banquet.

'She's got no womb,' Sandra used to say.

If women want to stop you fancying their sister they always tell you this. It really works. As an engineer you visualize the end of your penis hanging in space.

'They'd quarrelled, that's all it was,' David was saying. 'Sandra and the Belgian.' He was trying to make it seem not too bad that he had pissed up my life. Caroline said: 'I expect she just wanted to ask you how you are.'

'Oh yes. And she comes all the way from Belgium carrying her cases? Poor old Scottie must have been in a state that night. She needed me. We always said we could rely on each other. No matter whether we're together or not.' I was going to cry in a minute and I thought I'd got over all that.

Caroline said: 'That's what couples always say. Then a year later they're like strangers. Look at Brian when I went to collect my dog. Who? he said. Oh, Caroline! Come in! You'd never think we'd slept together, had about three abortions, been to Morocco. We slept in the desert with a flat tyre for two nights. Who? he said.'

'You've said all that,' David told her.

'When did she go back?' I asked David.

Caroline said: 'The same week you kicked Janet out. She went back to Brussels with Janet – they're sharing a flat.'

'The same flat in the Avenue Molière?'

David said: 'You won't let people talk about her. Of course you don't know anything. Anyway, he's got her back now. He's a real con-man. He'd been through half the British contingent of secretaries before Sandra fell for him.'

'How do you know that?'

'Never mind how. Look, you're getting upset again. When I saw you with that blonde bird at night school tonight I really thought you were over it. Now look at you. There's somebody at the door.'

'It's your mother,' Caroline said, without looking round.

In prisons you don't have to look round or think twice, you just have to put marks on the wall. Molly came smiling, wrinkled, but with a gay step and bright clothes; you can see the Tiller Girl inside the old lady. 'Hello, Alec. I knew you were here.'

Nobody questioned it. If you can smell the future you can certainly smell what's behind a wooden door. In any case my Chevvy was parked outside. I've got an American sedan as big as two lorries. I haven't had a chance to talk about it yet.

'Do you want some tea, Mum?' Caroline said.

Molly shivered, started taking little parcels in holly wrappings out of a leather shopping bag. 'No, I'll have a drop of your Christmas present.' David said: 'You haven't? Not already?' She said: 'There's only three weeks to go. I'll be glad when it's all over.' Nice, family things. Because I don't like prisons don't think I don't like families.

And she said: 'I've got your present, Alec.'

We saw each other perhaps twice a year and nobody knew I was coming to David's tonight. That is occult power.

'Don't unwrap it,' she said, giving me a small flat parcel. 'It's a cake plate with cherries on it.' This brought full attention from David and Caroline. Caroline said: 'A cake plate with cherries on it! Alec doesn't eat cake. Alec wears slimjim denims.' Molly just looked at me and I looked at Molly, took the parcel, humbly, you might say. A week before I had broken one of Sandra's cake plates with cherries on it. I had told nobody. Now David and Caroline were tuned in to us. Molly came and stood in front of me, looking serious.

'Somebody has come into your life, Alec. I've been getting vibrations for weeks. She's one of us.'

I said: 'Could it be Sandra?'

'I don't know,' Molly said. 'She's a witch. Sandra's not a witch, is she?'

'I don't know,' I said. You live with somebody for five years, and what do you really know?

Molly said: 'There's a lot of love and a strong smell of petrol – could you open the window, David? It's almost over-powering.'

I said: 'Perhaps Jacques Conte is going to be killed in a car crash and Sandra's coming home to me.'

Molly said: 'It could be that. There is a death. I wasn't going to tell you that. To tell you the truth I'm frightened.' She turned to Caroline. 'You're not in love with Alec, are you, Caroline? No, don't laugh. I have to know. David's talking about flying at Christmas. It could be an air crash. A lot of petrol.'

I said: 'Jets don't burn petrol. They burn paraffin. Jet kerosene.'

Caroline said: 'There's nothing between me and Alec. If David got killed in an air crash I'd marry Henry Lum. I think he's gorgeous.' Henry Lum is the estate agent she works for.

'That's all right, then,' Molly said.

Then she took her coat off. You will gather that this was not an unusual entrance for her to make. Sometimes all the lights went out. Conversation got back to normal; scandal. I asked David where he was flying at Christmas and he became secretive. He was involved in some kind of security business at the moment and had invented what he called stereophonic barking dogs. This is a way of guarding premises with loud-speakers.

'I don't know yet,' he said. Caroline shot him one implacable wife look. I always got the impression that by this time she hated nearly everything about him.

David put his arm round me in the street when he saw me off. 'Sorry about the play,' he said. 'I've really been waiting to get it off my chest for a long time. About that night. When Sandra came back. I couldn't tell you while you were still suicidal. Then tonight you had a different look about you.'

'I do feel different,' I said. I had not seen him since every-thing rhymed. He gave me another hug: 'Take care, mate.'

I tooted my horn as I drove away. It was eleven o'clock and a Thursday. I cried copiously all the way across north London. And then I thought, and I don't know why, for it came out of nowhere: propeller aircraft use petrol. The old Flying Fortress used petrol – lots of it. There was a crack like a gunshot. It seemed to come from the seat beside me. All there was there was Molly's Christmas present. The plate with cherries on it, still wrapped and labelled; the Sandra replacement. I felt it carefully – it had broken across the middle.

And then I was thinking about Morag, whom I had not met yet, which is what she wanted. I stopped crying and felt curiously comforted.

4

Tonight I want to talk about brain rhythms. Very exhausting to write at all after a day at Battersea Power Station. Tibbs was there. I do hate those chaps who have been doing the job for fifty years and know more than scientific instruments. I caught him dipping his finger in the boiler water and tasting it to see if my conductivity calibration was correct. Bloody savages; they hate progress. Half of my emergency calls are sabotage.

As you know, unless you accurately monitor and treat with ammonia the water that goes into £10 000 power station boilers they are very soon due for £10 000 replacements. Not only that, but men are losing their lives probing around inside in their inefficient gas-masks fighting the corrosion. I don't want to overstate how important (various aspects of) my job is, I just want to state it. People like Tibbs in their brown cowgowns and bicycle clips have been holding back this country for too long. We won't reach the new industrial revolution in a top hat and Union Jack waistcoat leading a bulldog. To reach the new automated world of leisure and travel and plenty, we have to pass through chaos. Growth will come through streamlining, men will be replaced by buttons. But men will still want wages before the buttons are properly connected, wages and prices will conflict, governments will fall.

Why?

It follows, doesn't it, that the democratic system of government is just as out-of-date as its burden; it, too, will be replaced by buttons. Westminster Palace will be a museum, like this one I live in, to the glory and the splendours and the agonies of the past. Come in, sir, come in, madam, you pays y'r tuppence and you comes in. No such museums in George Orwell's entertaining and brilliant *1984*. This is because George misread the signs, took the wrong path in the forest of evidence in which he wrote, dying from tuberculosis, the Flying Fortresses still limping home.

The inevitable future contains a fully automated world run by the chairman of the company with an élitist staff. The economy will be based, as now, on human needs, but the consumers will not participate, any more than pigs and cows clock in for work on the farm. This is the final solution because only happiness is stable. A slave society, a persecuted minority, any state of injustice is in perpetual strain.

Dust settles on the planet, the oceans are flat and from the foothills you measure the mountains.

How?

The answer lies in brain rhythm. I love you I love you I love fuck love fuck good dog woof kiss kiss kiss, the single creature in a single shell, the walls, the happy happy happy prison of love, kiss, fuck, love kiss fuck, hulloo! hulloo! hulloo! The little goodbye whistle on a descending third.

'What do you know about extra-sensory perception, Alec?' asked Ragusson. You remember Ragusson? Write him in blue in the margin.

We are nearly ready to begin the equation.

The Italian scientist Volta discovered electricity when he received a shock while dissecting a frog; long ago, in one of the old centuries. The volt, however, was not in Volta, it was in the frog. Poetry is in man, science is in God. He has given you a voltage and frequency and somewhere in Danzig is a man who knows how to plug you in – to HAP-PI-NESS.

Into a world where everything rhymes.

> You'll think this funny I suppose,
> I find I've got a crooked nose.
> It's late to find out something new
> But then my eyes are crooked too.
> Until I get another biff
> The world's gone straight –
> My face skew-whiff.

This is as much as I intend to say about brain rhythms for the present.

You'll be wanting to get on with the story. I have not left it. To show a relationship between any series of events it is necessary to create a climate, ambience, or at least a relevance of feeling; to give life, which is essentially amorphous, an appearance of unity and direction. What I dislike and mistrust in fiction, as opposed to reading technical books or biographies, and why it fails to hold my adult interest (children are content with distraction and escapism) is that the events seem to have logical order, precise significance, the story *unfolds*; the personae wait in the wings.

Not so with what I am trying to set down here. From the moment I set foot on the island, my Robinson Crusoe would have said, I had a very funny feeling. My story concerns a number of other very funny feelings that followed during the course of the next ten or eleven months. My island was sanctuary in the sea of depression, coming ashore after the crack-up, skin alive, senses acute and with a very strong overall feeling, the biggest very funny feeling of all, that I was not alone. I had seen the footprints but I had not yet seen Friday.

Somebody loved me, there was a smell of petrol and there was a death, past or future. According to Molly's nose. Engineers don't believe in this rubbish except at horoscope level; as entertainment, that is. Cracked plates they believe in. 'My daughter can do rather remarkable things,' Geoffrey said, didn't he? That sounds like fun.

She didn't foretell – Molly, I mean – anything about getting mugged in Long Acre in broad daylight. Show me a future that sounds like fun.

'What you doing for Christmas?'

This is Vicky talking. What the bloody hell has it got to do with her, you might ask. I've met her, how many times? Twice. Slept with her once. I called in at Danny's bar about two in the afternoon. Partly because nobody had invited me and also because I had a little appetite ticking away in my loins. I fancied an afternoon on the bed; thought I might take her home and buy her some more dog food. Her nipples were now pushing through a little hand-crocheted blue wool top, I think they call it. There were about five other men looking at her flesh.

'I don't know. When's Christmas? Nothing.' Sandra is Christmas to me and she's in Brussels. I said : 'What are you doing this afternoon?'

'Just a minute.' She went and looked after somebody else.

'And what are you doing this afternoon, Mr Ranger?' I looked around and there he was : Ragusson. 'Hello, Alec. Are you on your way to see me?'

'No.'

'We have a little deal to discuss,' he said. He had taken off his dark glasses to disarm me. I was surprised to find he's a plump businessman of about fifty.

'What do you mean – a contract for my book?'

'A contract for two books,' he said. 'Let me buy you a drink. What is it?'

'But I've only written one book.'

'Come to the office.' He started clicking his fingers to attract Vicky.

I said : 'If you've got a deal why haven't you written to me?'

'I am short-staffed. Geoffrey has got the flu.'

'Oh dear,' I said. 'Well, it can wait.'

Ragusson put on his glasses. He said : 'It can't wait. Have a drink with me and come back to the office.'

'I can't. I've got an appointment.' It was true; I had one call to make in Long Acre. I planned to do it while Vicky was finishing up and call back for her. He then noticed the case chained to my left wrist. I always chain Sandra's school satchel to my wrist in case I leave it somewhere. It would break my heart if I lost it. She brought it back from Lairg one day after one of her visits home. It is a tattered old fold-over leather briefcase and it has her name and form number in ink inside the flap. S. McP. V. It is one of the most treasured items in my museum. Jacques Conte will never get as far back into her girlhood as that. Scottie girls are genetically and nationally attached, lifelong; the man who keeps a firm grasp of their umbilical cord will always stand a chance. I can now play several of her school songs on her flageolet, for instance.

'Do you want a drink, Mr Ragusson?' Vicky was saying, all her busty blonde beauty framed in her noddy hole. Ragusson, however, was staring at my chained wrist still; I think it impressed him more than my book. 'What's in there? Money? Engineers don't earn that much money?'

'I'll have a lemonade,' I told Vicky. 'With ice.'

'What about tomorrow?' Ragusson said.

'Have you read my textbook?' I asked him.

The very thought pained him. 'I don't read books. It has been passed, accepted, scheduled for the autumn next year, price four-twenty, green covers, thirty-six illustrations. We shall want rough diagrams from you for our draughtsmen. Bring them with you tomorrow.'

He was doing that thing that people do who suspect they have been too friendly; he was now being too business-like. And talking rubbish. Geoffrey had all the illustrations in a separate folder. I didn't tell him. He is the kind of man who would remember to feel foolish when he found out; even more foolish because I had not bothered to correct him. As though, perhaps, engineers can't waste time with gangsters. To top it, when Vicky gave me my drink she said she would be ready at three. 'Excuse me,' Ragusson said. He walked away through the noddy arches to the lavatory or to Tonne's office.

'What you doing for Christmas, Alec?' said Goldilocks again. I put out my cigarette, drank my drink, touched her nipple, all with my right hand. 'Three o'clock,' I said.

I did not get back at three o'clock. Let me give you a word of advice. If you want to get back at three o'clock don't walk around Long Acre with a leather case chained to your wrist. Villains are inclined to get the wrong idea.

I was on my way back from Webster's when it happened. I mean the case was empty. It was just a convenient way of carrying a few boxes of buffer tablets. The trouble with being an electronics engineer, everything you mention about your job you've got to draw diagrams. Private eyes don't have this bother and nor do writers. Buffer tablets are what you dissolve in water to produce buffer solutions which are solutions of stable pH value into which you immerse – ah, shit. Webster's Photogravure use one of our instruments and they have to be standardized. It's like turning that little knob on your bathroom scales to set zero; then you hope the rest of the calibration is okay. Since drugs became a playground commodity our buffer tablets have been vanishing by the gross. They're poisonous, but nobody seems to die. 1 pH, for instance, is like very strong acid. At the other end of the scale, 11 pH would alkalize your giblets. Needless to say, which is why I'm about to say it, there's another Tibbs called Simpson at Webster's who checks all our scientifically standardized buffer tablets with a bit of litmus paper.

'That last lot was out, mate,' he said, this time; 'we ruined a couple of colour plates before we found out. . . .' Drop dead, Simpson. I've got a button to replace people like him. Friends of the fucking earth.

I was attacked about ten yards from Bow Street police station. There's a narrow street, a hundred narrow streets criss-crossing Long Acre, Bow Street, King Street – it's one of our early-morning places where she'd take me to buy flowers, three in the morning, drink coffee at the stall with tramps, child tramps that is, then sometimes round to Smithfield for a chunk of wholesale beefsteak; me and Sandra, in the long five years, and Moosh, victualling the prison, filling our lives with London. There, then, in that place that blossoms at dawn with daffodils and backing lorries and shouting men, where my Caledonian would cry: 'Alec! Loo' a' that! It's like a field in there! Hyacinths in December!' This, before the Garden moved south.

'Look out, mate!'

When this is said behind you the instinct is to flash a glance behind. In that moment somebody pushed a case of oranges on a trolley out from a wholesaler's doorway. As I put my hands out to save my face, the voice behind, which also had fists, pushed me forward so that I was folded neatly across the oranges. While imprisoned there, two men I could not see went to work on my chained briefcase, holding my arm outstretched like a log of wood ready for sawing. There was a good deal of pulling, painful pulling, at my chained wrist, then somebody said: 'I think we'll have to take his hand with it – got the chisel?'

'No!' I screamed. 'For God's sake! It's empty! It's not locked! Open it!'

They ignored me and freed the case, as I discovered later, by breaking loose one end of the leather handle to which it was attached; the leather handle first worn smooth by Sandra's little hand to and from school. When they broke and ran I was able to count them; I could have sworn there were six: there were two. Three. I was tripped up as I started after them, cracked my face on the pavement. As an engineer, this is the kind of retribution I can do without. I'm sure when this stranger rolled me over my face must have looked rather like Geoffrey's did to me after I'd tripped him.

'Dear dear! Dear dear! It's Mr Ranger, isn't it?'

You remember Tonne of the dark visage? Danny? Half Irish and half Irish? Ragusson's Belgian translator of Russian and German? This was the first time I heard him speak; he sounded like a real Mick.

'What the hell happened?' he said. And as he helped me to my feet, saw the dangling stainless-steel chain, he hazarded: 'Have you been tied up?' I won't waste your time as he was trying to waste mine while his friends escaped. The police station was the nearest possibility to getting my prize exhibit back, but Tonne stopped me.

'Don't go there in person,' he advised. 'If you do you'll wait half an hour to see somebody, another half an hour getting a statement down and then it will be filed in lost property. You'll hear no more. Get them on the telephone and it goes to crime squad – they'll be out searching in five minutes. There's a telephone in here – come on, Mr Ranger.'

Come on, Snowy! Come on, Jock! Come on, Dick Barton!

Tonne took me into yes, you may have guessed it, Ragusson's office; full of technical books, technical publications, old Ralph the production manager, Joan the secretary and the smell of oranges, oranges, oranges from below. Ragusson stood up from behind his desk and smiled.

'You decided to come, then? Good!'

On the wall behind him was a two-foot colour portrait of Vicky, naked with her thighs apart, examining her own vagina with a mirror. It reminded me of my date with her, but I was too intent on getting Sandra's school case back to worry about it. It was pretty apparent that Danny's bar and Ragusson's technical publications firm was a pretty closed shop. Tonne told Ragusson what had happened and the Fiking Publisher got the police very efficiently. Too efficiently, as I gradually worked out. He handed me the receiver across the desk:

'Here, Alec. Tell them all about it.'

You know how you collect things in a briefcase, turning your inside pockets out into it every time your jacket or coat gets a pregnant bulge; all the things you can't put away in a drawer somewhere because you need them, yet you never need them. Look in your pockets now; what have you got? Well, that's what I've got in this precious school satchel of Sandra's, plus the love letter she wrote me from Brussels the day before she slept with Jacques Conte in her Avenue Molière bedroom on the fourth or fifth floor at the rear with the bloody door shut.

'What kind of letter?' the policeman's voice asked on the phone. Does it matter what kind of letter? Well, yes; if the thieves turf everything out of the case, the contents, being of even less intrinsic value than the case, something might be found somewhere. The comical thing was I'd read it so many hundred times, had cried over it, shown it to passers-by at one stage, that I was able to quote Sandra's letter whole; comical because Ragusson's Oliver Hardy deadpan eye was fixed on me while I recited it, as if to say, but why chained to your wrist?

'Dear Alec – '

'What?'

'That's my name. Alec Ranger. Dear Alec, I've just put the phone down so I feel you're very close – I love you and miss you and wish you were here –

'My girl-friend Sandra. This is one of her letters in the case. Small purple handwriting on small blue notepaper. I have two single beds in my room at the pension and it seems a pity that the other is empty when you could be here and – what?'

'Bring it in, sir – '

'I haven't got it – it's in the case.'

'Allow me,' said Ragusson. He leaned over and took the telephone from me. 'Jim. It is me. Mr Ranger is very upset. It happened just under my office here. Put the word round the man mugged in Covent Garden at three this afternoon is a friend of mine.' To me, Ragusson said : 'Describe the case.'

'It's an ordinary cheap brown leather school satchel, envelope shape, three compartments, corrugated sides, brass lock in the middle of the flap, two buckle-type fixing straps, one buckle broken off and oh yes, her name written in ink inside the flap, on the rough, light-coloured back-side of the leather – Sandra McPh – no, S. McPh. V – the "vee" is for standard five.'

'Did you get all that, Jim?'

From Tonne's very grave face and the very grave faces of Joan and old Ralph I got the feeling that London, in the form of an important London publisher's office and an important London police station, was pausing to consider the case of the violent robbery of a child's school satchel with nothing in it. I also got the strong feeling, meaningless though it might appear, that it had been set up. That when Ragusson strode off leaving me and Vicky at the bar, he strode off to set it up; the attack, the robbery, followed by this dragnet. Could he possibly suppose there might be something valuable in the case? That middle-aged electronics engineers don't chain their girl-friend's school satchel to their wrist from pure besotted sentiment. Try to work it out for yourselves, remembering always the Viking's capacity for comedy and that his master-mind plots – it seemed to me at that time before the murder – were never likely to be any more demanding of one's intelligence than one of Hal Roach's Laurel and Hardy mini-dramas.

'Okay, Sergeant, we'll remember you at Christmas. Bye now.' The fat clown hung up, then looked at me with narrowed,

Mexican- bandit voracity. 'Ees okay, *señor*. Donna worry. Your possessions weel be recovered and the miscreants incarcerated with a blunt knife!'

'Oooo! Mr Ragusson!' Joan shrieked. This was part of her job to shriek and giggle at Ragusson's sallies.

The moment was diffused by some slight clicking going on in my memory bank. The Mexican bandit act had something to do with it, particularly 'incarcerated with a blunt knife' – this was so much the Poly humour of the early fifties it was like a time shift; corny, wretched reminder of your age group, a sharp example for those stuck for ever with their childhood vocabulary. Phrases like 'all that jazz' and trend words like 'hopefully', 'surely', coined as monuments to inanity and branded on the stupid for all time. There are no clichés in the automated world.

Incarcerated with a blunt knife? Who said that? What character from Elec and Mag hides inside those rolls of Oliver Hardy obesity? And how did Geoffrey and Ragusson come together? And who is Joan . . . ? Watch this screen, folk. Now I'm doing it. Every time I do that, skip a page. Or turn to the diagrams, explanatory notes and basic formulae. I have asked the publisher to put them under tissue paper on facing page like a latter-day Cruikshank. In case he chickens on this besides the unjustified typescript litho I have requested and the facsimile of my associate membership certificate of the Institute of Electrical Engineers which I want instead of an author picture, here is my thumbnail portrait of Mum-one and Mum-two in the Ragusson office – Joan Broonzy and Ralph Iddle. Incidentally and before I forget it the nude of Vicky examining her vagina with a mirror is advertising *Know Your Body* and tops Ragusson's medical list of books; yet another example of the Birkbeck esoterics fringing across the road on to Charing Cross Road porno stalls.

'How's your face?' the publisher asked, suddenly, as if aware that the audience was tired of the pantomime. 'Take Mr Ranger to first-aid, Joan.'

'I'm all right,' I told him. The orange box had treated my face more kindly than the pavement had treated Geoffrey's.

Only later did I begin to connect the two incidents; only after what seemed like free circumstance connected with a master-plan. Each time I tried to kick the scene I got kicked back. Joan took my chin in her motherly hand and rotated my face to the light. 'Yes, come on, let me dab it for you, Mr Ranger.' I kept telling them I was all right but I got led away.

'You can get lock-jaw,' old Ralph said.

Joan Boonzy is a big blonde woman of about forty who makes up like a circus front, though her typing is so good you can print it. Her enunciation is the 'oa, yais', cockney kind which I won't detail. I prefer to draw diagrams and project dimensions from salient corners.

Among all the 'oa yais's' then and 'does it smart, dears' in the little first-aid room – which is also a photographic dark room – Joan suddenly said, while rubbing TCP cream on a graze : 'Heard from Morag lately?'

Morag is one of those singular names about which one never has to query 'Morag who?' How many Morags have you had in your life?

'Why should I hear from Morag?'

'You were always one of her favourites, Mr Ranger. She's always on about her dad. There! Now look in the mirror. Doesn't that look better. No nasty old germs . . .'

And so on and so on and so on while I am examining a part of the equation that doesn't make sense. It registered swiftly enough, as ever; I couldn't believe that what I had understood Joan Boonzy to say was what she meant. She went on putting away the medicants and I was watching soles of feet and skirts and shadowy female crutches passing overhead through an oblong of green thick corrugated glass, the room being in the basement, under the orange warehouse. It is sometimes better to wait for something else to follow complete mystery; any light is light in utter darkness.

'She was on form this morning, all right!'

'Who was?'

'Young Morag. Look what she did to this.' She put her finger on a crack in the wall mirror which had been cutting my reflection in two. I knew instinctively that it had not been hit with a brick. 'That's why Geoffrey went home. Old Bony sent him to look for her. He was so excited! Well, that's what he's been waiting for, the big stuff. It went off like a cannon! Funny thing was, everybody heard it but nobody knew what had happened. You see they have this little blind pulled down when they're doing D & P. That's why the taps are painted black though it's dreadfully unhealthy for Arthur – up a ladder one week, black hole of Calcutta the next.'

'Joany! Joany!' came Ralph's voice from upstairs. Every time a door opened you got oranges. As his footsteps clattered down towards us, Joan pressed my shoulder, secretively: 'We don't tell *him* everything.' And then, quickly, remembering the start of our conversation: 'You haven't heard from her then?'

I said, equally conspiratorially: 'No. Not for about three weeks.'

'Nothing valuable, I hope?' she said.

'A plate,' I said. Her expression of polite relief coincided with Ralph's entrance, but she went on as one does to simulate normal conversation: 'It's not natural, is it? I mean it must be much worse for you, her father.'

'Yes,' I said, my head full of dark lights.

'He wants you to run off two copies of Mr Ranger's book contract,' Ralph told Joan. She said: 'Okeydoke!' and went out. Ralph held me back for a moment:

'Vicky's been on the blower, Mr Ranger.' He whispered, pointing upstairs with a dramatically stiff finger: 'Don't mention what you're doing for Christmas . . .'

Ralph is about five feet ten inches, lives in Notting Hill; his sister was one of the prostitutes murdered by Christie. I'll describe him more fully when things are less confusing.

Let us get back to the equation, which is what it's all about, whether you are God the scientist or God the engineer. You will notice that without any effort on my part a number of factors have been added, subtracted, multiplied, whichever way you calculate. I am now Morag's father, for instance. This might be true or false. Go into any little morass – and old friends are most representative – and something is going to stick. Especially if you had it away with his wife before he did.

Sandra McPherson hated one thing about me and my life; the number of little morasses which were still adhering. Add one brain-damaged daughter and the chances of Sandra returning from Brussels to our cage are zero. I have a dream that I shall be perched and whistling on a bough when she comes back and I shall take her a bright, coloured feather. I love you, I love you, I love you, I shall whistle in musical thirds descending. And she'll tell me that she loves me and will take the feather and start a new nest. Because I know that no other man could love her in his whole lifetime as much as I love her every minute; that she can never be a part of his life one tiny fraction as much as she was a part of our life together. You will be pleased to know that I am coming to the part where we plan to kill Jacques Conte, the Belgian author, so that Sandra can come home. This may not sound like rational or Christian behaviour now, but when you hear what he has to say about me and my life with Sandra in his beastly newspaper column and in his books you will agree that what happened was inevitable in the name of justice.

Equation-wise, then, we have several new factors which may very well cancel in the working out. Here at East Finchley tech we used the 'J' notation for such a purpose. Defined as the square root of minus-one, 'J' denotes a phase change which may effect various values of the equation during its working out but is cancelled out at the end; therefore 'J' is a lubricator. Add it to both sides to facilitate and clarify and then get rid of it. Assuming an ordinary reader's knowledge of vectorial algebra, you will know that any instantaneous voltage may be made up of several out-of-phase components; plus or minus 'J' will indicate the nature and amplitude of these.

Now, in a world where everything rhymes and the breeze riffles the fine hairs on your scalp, where the deep subconscious is in tune with the cosmos, the human elements fall into place and assume their true value and phasing as neatly as any electrical equation. There are no tangles in a straight line. To gather information it was going to be necessary to talk to

Geoffrey Neasden again and to get a new battery for my miniature pocket wire recorder. Most of the conversations I have written here in this report were secretly recorded at the time. There is no other possible way that people can remember what has been said except in essence. Try putting down some of your quite recent conversations to demonstrate the truth of this. Now compare it with any dialogue in a top-of-the-chart novel. I am talking, of course, about first-person writing.

I listened, more or less unblinking, then, to the incredible revelations from Joan Boonzy, but no more so, I would think, than the revelations one would have received from quite humble minions in some exalted top-secret wartime establishment. The milkman, for instance, must have known precisely when D Day was going to be; and how long they expected to be gone. I discovered from that same recorded talk that everyone seemed to take Morag Neasden's extraordinary powers for granted, that Ragusson was waiting for them to develop so that he could corner her power for a secret weapon, either for patriotism or profit, that Arthur the window-cleaner, once Morag's long-haired boy-friend (and possibly Joan's son), now did developing and printing in Ragusson's dark room and that Ragusson himself – astoundingly for me – is none other than old Bony from the Poly (Rag and Bones, get it?), son of that famous Oslo mayor who started the Christmas tree habit in our Trafalgar Square.

So the pieces assembled coming up to Christmas, without any particular shape or pattern yet becoming apparent.

Christmas is always a bad time in Sandraland. It's not that you have any more wonderful time in prison, it's just that you remember it more. I usually cry a lot at Christmas and so does Moosh. I suppose everybody does. When you think about it you only get about seventy. If you're very lucky five of them are wonderful.

'What you doing for Christmas?' Vicky said for about the hundredth time. We are in Dingwall's disco at Camden Lock and she is dressed in a little bunny-rabbit fur with her nipples like a pair of gnome eyes peeking at the top and long red-tighted legs right up on the table almost. Her hair is gleaming platinum and her eyes decorated up like a pair of bedroom slippers, her lips pout and glisten as if about to do what they were doing last night on my museum bed. I'm beginning to like her because there's no fear of settling down with her any more than you would settle down with a pantomime. Speaking as an engineer, she is almost entirely replaceable. Not so Janet with her Scottie accent and brandy and Babycham. I got rid of her just in time; another month and the cell door would have been shut. Sandra on the outside for ever. I have been very depressed since losing her school satchel; as though I have started to let go. 'You don't want to stay in that bloody place for Christmas,' she said. 'You know what you'll be like. Playing that record, walking up and down, getting drunk. That little dog ought to get away, Alec . . .' Vicky still talking.

The gist of it is, to keep it short, she wants me to drive her and her Great Dane home to Suffolk for Christmas so that she can be with her mum and young brothers and sisters. She can't go on the train or by bus with the dog. She was crying about it last night, all her eyes melting away over everything. I don't want a girl that cries. I'm the one that cries. The heart-broken engineer needs a cheerful girl who distributes the profits. She doesn't need a family or a dog. On the other hand, to be fair, Vicky has got a lot of the things she needs. The cheerful girl, I mean.

'You can't shut a dog away for Christmas, can you?'

You tell Sandra that. She must know that I'm alone.

'Of course I would share the petrol.'

'How's your drink?'

'You'd like my mum.'

Dingwall has got the longest bar in London, though it still seems tiny once a girl gets an idea in her head. The night Sandra decided to move in with me I left her sitting at that same table; instead of going to the lavatory I left the building to go home, pack a case and leave the country. I was free for the first time since I left school, families had dispersed. Barbara was happy in Nassau – did I want to put the irons on again?

We had been going around for about a month since Sandra arrived from America, her divorce was not yet through, she could still hear grating demanding voices, 'When do we eat?' We had made love inexpertly at a country hotel. Sandra had changed her mind too late and during the struggle for possession the bedside telephone had got knocked off its hook and the night porter had got the rest of our steaming night in his ear. Walking up Chalk Farm Road that night I decided that Sandra had as much freedom to lose as I did and I walked back, repaid entrance money, joined her at the table. She had been a little worried, but had not moved, smiled at me, fluttered her eyelashes, said: 'Do you like this tune?'

That was the tune I keep playing when I want to die. It was a Donovan number that came around the same time as 'Mellow Yellow'. This one's called 'Sunshine Superman' and we danced to it. Sandra was a very stylish dancer, had a little trick of going up on her toes and freezing the movement for a beat, moved her body and arms and legs as if she was weaving her way through a jungle of fronds, underwater, dreaming and dreaming. I held her in my arms and didn't let go for five years when she said: 'Do you mind if I go and temp in Brussels for a few weeks, Alec? You can come too. . . .'

'John wants you to go to Brussels, doesn't he?' Vicky said now. Who's John? 'John Ragusson. He was talking about it in his sleep.' A line like this, listened to on the wire recorder afterwards, for this was about the time I decided to get out my report, the footprints in the sand getting deeper by the day, Girl Friday cracking mirrors, a line like this tells you how little you've been listening. I did not know that Ragusson's first name is John. I did not know that he was screwing Vicky, that he was the married lover paying her room rent. I did not know that Ragusson wanted me to go to Brussels or that he talked in his sleep.

'Isn't that Arthur?' Vicky exclaimed suddenly. 'That's Arthur. Yoo-hoo, Arthur!'

A young man whom we had both plainly seen cavorting at our end of the long bar for the past hour, that is dancing on his own, sometimes an eccentric sort of charleston, sometimes supporting himself by his hands on the counters either side and doing a tap dance with his dangling legs, sometimes dancing across the room with a tray of drinks, now looked at us and gave a camp wave: 'Yoo-hoo to you-hoo too-hoo! Hi, knickers!' He then had an extra exaggerated take on me and came mincing across, smiling like a girl.

'Hello,' he said, in a musical camp voice. Quite pleasant and friendly, but queer as a cuckoo. He knew me well. 'It's Alec Ranger, isn't it? Now, you tell me how I know. I recognized you from right across there. No, don't guess. You never will, anyway. You're the spitting image of your daughter! Isn't he like his daughter, Vicky? You know, Geoff's girl, young Morag. Blimey, no wonder she's got an affinity with you – you heard about the mirror? What a scream! I told her, "You'll be knocking down buildings next!" Well, she could! If she can do one thing she can do another. Mind you, she shouldn't be stuck out there in that old aeroplane with all those skeletons, should she? Do you think so, honestly, Mr Ranger? It's ever so damp in the winter – just a minute, I've got a customer. Now don't go, I'll mix you two of my specials. Oo, it is nice seeing you, Mr Ranger. Wait till I tell her! She'll crack another plate! Here – she's cracked everything in this bloody place. Don't say anything. I have to keep sticking 'em together! Well, they'd have a fit if they knew! Think I was barmy – oh, just a minute – Coming!'

Arthur Boonzy trotted back to his job, holding his hands like petals, did a pirouette at the bar and trotted back at the same pace, in time with the music, having thought of something else:

'It was that apple!' He pointed to the big red apple on the front of my mauve T-shirt. I had duplicated most of the clothes that Morag pinched. I couldn't get the same colour apple.

He said: 'That really suited her. I hemmed up the trousers and took in the jacket. It's the nicest I've ever seen that girl look. They all thought so.'

I said: 'She doesn't live there alone, then?'

'Wart!' cried a voice from the bar.

'Eh?' he said, distracted. 'Oh no. Well, you know, we come and go. See you in a minute, loves.'

We watched him trip back to the bar and Vicky said: 'Doesn't he go on? I like him, though. He doesn't take any nonsense from John Ragusson. Doesn't he remind you of somebody? An actor – I'll think of it in a minute. Bit of an old woman. What will you do then, Alec?'

'What?'

'For Christmas?'

Either I was going mad or the world was. Nobody found it unusual, a young girl living with a bomber full of skeletons in a wood. Nobody commenting on Geoffrey's daughter getting transferred to me. Nobody found it remarkable, her power of mind over matter projected at long distance. Everybody obsessed with their own problems. Either that or the situation was so old it was not news any more.

'How long has Morag been visiting this Flying Fortress?' I asked Vicky. She said: 'Oh, a long time. Years.' I said: 'Do the authorities know about it?' She said: 'She can do as she likes now she's over sixteen.' I said: 'What do you mean?' She said: 'Morag came out of care the year after Geoffrey came out of prison. That was two years after the accident. Nobody talks about it now. It wasn't very fair on him. He never touched her. Anyway, she's not his own daughter.'

None of this answered my second question. I tried again: 'Who found the Flying Fortress?'

She seemed vague about it, as though she had been told by somebody who had been told by somebody else. 'Morag did, I think. It belongs to her. They say she's made a nice garden round it.'

I said, patiently: 'But why didn't the American Air Force take it away? Give the crew a proper burial?' She said: 'I don't know. I don't suppose they know anything about it. Why should they? Findings keepings. Look at that girl's dress.'

Instead I looked at Vicky and sipped my scotch. Her name is Victoria Meadows. If you opt for her you opt for her dog and for the dubious freedoms of a Chalk Farm prison and the big questions never get answered. Ever. The footprints stay on the sand and the coconuts remain on the trees. You sink into the scented flesh every night and get tea in bed every morning and the love of your life is a distant dream buried in a distant wood.

5

Raymond came in. My fat son from Somerset House. The tax man. You never really know how your kids are going to turn out. I started him right, he can never blame me. By five he knew Ohm's Law and a year later Lenz's Law and Faraday's Law. In this life, these are the only laws you're ever likely to need. The first governs the relationship between voltage, power, current and resistance. The second takes care of the closed circuit cutting lines of force – induction, in other words. Faraday governs condensers, capacitors if you like and electrostatics. Combine the three and you have those great leaping God-peaks of resonance that circle the earth and bridge continents and bounce off planets; harnessed by man for such things as Radio One Club.

'What are you doing for Christmas, Dad?'

He's a little tubby man with a pigeon-chested strut and a coconut hair style, the point or tuft being at the front as if constantly pulled around by his superiors (of which there are many). Sometimes he's got a full beard, sometimes not, and I can never remember after he's gone which way it was. He wears Billy Bunter eyeglasses through which he shafts highly critical barbs of wit and suspicion at you. He did it now, stalking round the room, sniffing.

'What's that stink?'

'That's Vicky's perfume.'

'Oh God. Not another. Is she living with you, then?'

'No and she's not going to.'

'That's what you said about Janet.'

'And I kicked her out.'

'That's what you said about Sandra. I thought you were going to preserve all her smells? Wearing off, is it? Good.' He came and watched me eating a kipper; it was the night I was taking my wire recorder out to Wembley to see Geoffrey. 'What were you doing in Oxford Street yesterday? Irma saw you and she said you were smiling and talking to yourself.' This was obviously one of the two or three reasons he had called in. If somebody close had died Raymond would wait until he'd got two or three more good reasons for calling; he has to work in columns. I don't know how he ever caught Irma who is a Dutch-Javanese jungle queen with masses of black hair, languorous eyes, high cheekbones, passionate lips, pineapple breasts; I think he caught her in a tax trap while she was still new to the country.

'What time was it?' I said.

'I don't know. She was in a bus at Oxford Circus.'

'Oh yes. I was doing my Christmas shopping. I may be going away.' I had no intention of going away but the announcement gets you off about a hundred family hooks.

'So are we,' he said. 'If you've got any presents I'd better take them now.' He laughed and rubbed his chubby hands. 'I hope you haven't been foolishly generous, Dad.' I went on eating my kipper. He said: 'We should make Valladolid this year.' He was following Napoleon's march across the Iberian peninsula, Christmas by Christmas. And he said: 'What were you laughing at in Oxford Street?'

I said: 'I was trying to persuade Morag to break some of those enormous plate-glass windows in the stores.'

'Who's Morag?'

'My daughter,' I told him.

He didn't blink an eye, quite prepared to believe anything; ready to accept brothers and sisters he hadn't heard about before. 'Irma said you were alone.'

'I know. That's the great thing about Morag.' I was beginning to toss her powers around like everybody else, making light of it, bathing in reflected glory, borrowing her eccentric plumes. I told Raymond everything I knew or thought I knew: Geoffrey, the Poly, Joyce who was about to have an abortion as Raymond's mother was about to have Caroline but married Geoffrey instead, presumably; about Ragusson, Tonne, Joan, Arthur, the Flying Fortress and its crew; about Morag's psychic powers. I got it all in and ate the kipper while he was still blowing out his cheeks and formulating an expert's opinion.

'Well, if it's really true, Dad,' he said at last, 'you may be able to claim retrospective tax benefit.'

And this was a boy, the only boy I had, sadly enough, who could tell you, aged eight and a half, that there are one thousand and fifty-five ergs in a British Thermal Unit.

'How well do you know Jacques Conte?' Raymond said then. This must be about four things he had come to see me about. I had not quite forgiven him for his attitude when I got back from Brussels with Cyril Dyball the policeman, a total stranger who happened to be sitting in the next seat in the Trident both going over and coming back. He and David Ballantine and Janet all flapping hot towels and brandy at me, my son cold and therapeutic. 'Put her right out of your mind, Dad. She's outgrown you and that's all there is to it. If you will have young girls, of course they're going to leave you. You're just a stepping-stone to them, an experience, something to look back on. That hard-eyed Scot wants more out of life than you can offer. Forget her, get back to work, find somebody your own age – either that or take an overdose. Don't hang on boring everybody else to death. And don't forget your tax returns. . . .'

I told Raymond that I didn't know Jacques Conte at all. I met him briefly once. He walked in on us after that terrible flight. I had been crying on Sandra's lap, begging her to come back to prison. The funny thing was, when I stepped out of the taxi – this police detective got me the taxi – there was Sandra up on the roof, waving down. It seemed too good to be true considering how she had shouted and raved at me on the telephone, trying to stop me going, telling me not to intrude. Then when the little buzzer went and she said the intercom was out of action and she would have to go down and find out who it was – then I realized she had been up on the roof waiting for her fucking author; hoping she would have time to warn him off.

'Well, he knows you, Dad,' said Raymond. What he had was a copy of the glossy review and topic magazine, *Books and Bookmen* – Sandra used to take it. It's very boring if you don't like books. The article was headed 'Sandra and the Dragon' and it was about the way this romantic, cultured, imaginative, understanding, warm and loving Continental male novelist rescued a Scots lass from a dull, fully-automated Englishman.

'I shouldn't read it if I were you,' Raymond said. 'He says you were a terrible lover. You bought her an electric vibrator to use until you came to bed.'

I felt quite angry. All her friends would read this. Writing is a very unfair weapon to use against an engineer; all I can do is blow him up. Get Morag to break his plates. During my crack-up period, when I knew Sandra was not coming back to me, that it was not simply an infatuation, that she was not merely getting her Continental urges out of her system, that she was on, in fact, the next phase of her life; during that time I planned to kill Jacques Conte several times and in very careful detail. I once went so far as to organize an alibi with David Ballantine so that I could cross the Channel with a forged passport and nip back after the murder. David went along with all those things because he knew that when it came to buying tickets I would not be up in time.

'If you had bothered to go over with her, spend a couple of weeks in Belgium, Sandra would still be here,' David used to say. It was a rotten thing to say because it was true. To the engineer, the Belgians had nothing to offer.

'Sandra wanted children and you were busy putting people out of work,' Raymond went on, remorsely. 'You put twelve thousand people on the dole in one year.' That was the year I worked on the Post Office sorter, which does everything except walk down the street whistling, and we're working on that. 'In Belgium they're still using horses on the land,' Raymond said. That's a waste of dog food. Raymond had not finished quoting Sandra's boy-friend.

'He says all the time she lived with you you were experimenting on her. Trying to feed brain rhythms back into her brain. Negative feed-back for people. Is that true?'

Once, that's the only time I tried it on Sandra. All great advances have had their distaff side. It's a woman's job to help her man. Especially when he's working for progress. I got an eight-channel electro-encephalogram of her brain recorded at Webster's laboratory, then built a resistance-capacity simulator and applied it to her head while she was asleep. It was no more uncomfortable than wearing rollers. The idea is delightful in its simplicity. Instead of putting out vibrations in search of constant stimuli, the brain becomes contented with itself. It's been done in Russia and in America; wherever there's a big change-over from man to machine in progress negative feed-back would be invaluable. A non-productive, non-participative consumer population would sit happily watching blank screens; no need to waste money on television fodder. This is one of the things Ragusson is after for his technical list.

'You stopped her writing poetry,' Raymond said. That was the only repeatable result. I needed more time, more instrumentation, a better and more docile subject. He said : 'She's started writing it again now.' He watched me making a note in my research notebook. Shafts of criticism coming from his piggy little eyes. The new man, properly treated, will no longer need family.

'You've got two soft spots, Dad,' Raymond said. 'In your head, I mean. Sandra and that mongrel.'

When he'd gone I kicked Moosh just to prove I could do it. Al'k! Al'k! Al'k! she said. Then I made a fuss of her. Once everything starts to rhyme and you feel the chill breeze on your skin and the fine hairs move on your scalp, you cannot be a fully-automated man any more. If I could do one more nasty thing and get my Scottie lass home again, I'd give it up.

'Yes, yes, yes,' said Morag inside my head. I have this supernatural assistant. The nasty thing was murder.

Revelations.
Start to cross-multiply, subtract, divide out and you find

that Geoffrey Neasden murdered his wife. His daughter (my daughter, Ragusson's daughter, your daughter if you went to Northampton Poly in the early fifties) had her revenge by accusing him of rape. This is Wembley, Middlesex, home of the Cup Final.

'I, ahem, didn't like to say anything,' he coughed and spluttered in his well-known, self-deprecating way. 'Well, I didn't want to offend you. I think she is your daughter, in fact, Alec. Sorry about that.'

I don't know how people write novels when drama emerges like this, over a cup of tea. When I suggested a scotch on the strength of this momentous bit of news it was typical of Geoffrey that he got it out of the medicine chest in the bathroom. 'Tell me about it,' I said. If Sandra had known about this extra bit of my past she would have finished long before she did. If she found out about it now she'd never come back. When I say now I mean then – we're still talking about last Christmas.

'I'd rather not,' Geoffrey said. 'It was so silly. I wanted Morag to go in for a university education and her mother didn't, that's all. I mean, she was brilliant, Alec. Any sacrifice would have been a terrific investment.' He looked round, apologetically. 'We wouldn't be living here.' You could see the way his mind worked and why somebody like Joyce would object. He said: 'Botany, chemistry, biology, something-mantics – she knew them all. She could distil insecticide poisons from plant life at eleven. What a waste.'

You began to see his own compassionate view of his daughter's brain damage. There's no money in cracking plates.

'If she wants to be a ballet dancer she can be a ballet dancer, Joyce used to say. Morag wanted to be a ballet dancer. With all that brain! You know what sort of girls are ballet dancers, Alec. Covent Garden is full of 'em. Most of 'em typists or flogging salt-beef sandwiches. Even the ballerinas don't bring home any money. Vicky, you know young Vicky, she's a ballerina. Nice girl, I like her, but anybody can have her on a Thursday before Danny pays her.'

People like Geoffrey trample all over your ego. If you

remember it was Thursday when Vicky first came to me with all that sympathy. On the Wednesday I had bought her dog food.

'Funny thing was Joyce always treated Morag as if she was her daughter and not mine. "This is my daughter," she used to say to people. Morag was the same. Ahem. Very funny feeling there was between us. Even when she was small I didn't like putting her in the bath or on the pottie, things like that. Nature's very strange, Alec. And when she started to grow up and wear little dresses she used to turn me on. If she came into our bed her mother always put her on the other side. Joyce used to watch me like a hawk. Her own father. Well, that's what I thought. I started to get really furtive. I was trying for an exterior B.Sc. at the time, but I couldn't concentrate. Do you want some more tea or some whisky?'

I had tea to make him feel better.

'Not only that,' he said. 'The little devil used to do it for the purpose. Try to provoke me. At twelve years old Morag was very provocative. They sent her home from school once – that came out in court, luckily. You couldn't have seen the papers. The *News of the World* was full of it. Whole page. Father sleeps with daughter after mother's death. Ahem. Not very nice, is it? I wanted to move away but I couldn't even sell the house. Fortunately they're nearly all black round here now. What's it like where you live?'

'When did you find out the truth?'

Geoffrey thought about it for a moment and I thought he was about to cry; he did his Laurel and Hardy head scratch. Then he sniffed and drank some tea. I was not enjoying stirring it all up but hell, I was in it too now. He said: 'That day. Day she died. We were on the way back from town. London University. That place the end of Store Street. We took Morag for her university entrance interview. Well, preliminary. She was only, what, fourteen or fifteen. When's her birthday?'

'April the twenty-fifth,' I said. We looked at each other, blankly. I said: 'How the hell do I know that?' Geoffrey laughed. 'Well, you're her father. That's what she thinks.

She's communicating, isn't she? Joan told me about the plate. He suddenly warmed and animated as if digressing on to something he knew altogether more about, like horse-racing. 'You know, Alec, quite honestly, never mind this and that, who's her dad and who isn't, mind over matter, Flying Fortresses and anterior lobes and so on, what really and truthfully worries me is this : suppose she missed one day and broke something really valuable?'

'What?'

'Something that cost a lot of money. Supernatural powers don't carry third-party insurance. I mean, take your clothes. I can't pay for those. She knows that. Now suppose she cracked a rare Ming dynasty vase in the British Museum? No don't laugh, she could do it. I mean it could cost a million pounds! And who would they come to? In a way I'm glad I'm not her legal father.'

Geoffrey had the goodness to dwell for a moment on this fact and realized where it might put me. He said : 'Well, of course, you're not either. At least, it hasn't been made official. But the thing is this, Alec. I think you could stop her doing it. I think you could talk to her. I think she would listen to you. Stop going there.'

'Stop going where?'

'To the Fort. That's where she does her bombing. Didn't you know? I thought you were talking to Arthur the other night? Yes, she sits in the bomb-aimer's seat, presses the bomb release – she has to concentrate on what she wants to hit. But anyone can make a mistake, Alec.'

'She could knock a building down,' I said.

'Oh no. She's tried that. She's tried every fucking thing starting with Buckingham Palace. No, she can only crack china. Thank God. Thank God, Alec! Christ, I don't mind paying for a few plates.'

'What about the mirror?'

'What mirror?'

'The mirror in Ragusson's dark room.' As soon as I told him I knew I should not have told him. They had all kept it away from him. No, they hadn't. Joan had told me that's why he had rushed off home. He was trying to keep it away from me. All the guilt lay in his weak little face and he started ahemming at top speed. He had decided to fob me off with my new responsibilities believing that Morag could only break china. Hide the fearful truth that her power was growing.

'I forgot about the mirror,' he said. 'Still. It's like china. In a way. That could be produced by the same anterior lesion. I don't think that's anything to worry about, Alec. Except the seven years' bad luck and I'm not superstitious. I don't suppose you are, either. We're both scientists after all. I hear you got your contract signed? Good. Make a nice textbook, that will. It's your first, isn't it? Ahem. I've been all through available literature. There's nothing else on automatic control treated in just that way. You know what it reminds me of? Lancelot Hogben. Remember *Mathematics for the Million*? Old Carson was furious when he found we were using it instead of the *Oxford*. . . .'

Geoffrey went on until he thought he had changed the subject and then I said:

'So that's china and glass. All she wants now is concrete and steel.'

'And wood,' Geoffrey said. 'Don't forget wood.'

'What about plastic?' We pondered plastics as we might have pondered the importance of a hundred-yard sprint to a long distance Olympiad. He said: 'I don't think she'd bother.'

I don't know whether I can convey to you how well I had fitted into this miracle scene. The rest were old hands and already I was beginning to feel like an old hand. Think of it this way: Christ's disciples were old hands, weren't they? Do you think they were astonished every time He performed another miracle? 'Look, J.C. We're getting tired of bread and fishes. Can you do something else?' When He made the dead man walk they were watching to see whether he walked with a limp.

Morag's crockery act was a kind of mutual amenity now.

'There's only one reason she's trying to extend her range,' Geoffrey said. 'It's this new road bridge they're thinking of building across the rivers at Harwich. It's going right through her wood. Of course she wouldn't hurt anybody. She's always very careful about that. She would crack it before anything got on it.'

'What, a bridge?'

There was a pause while he considered whether or not to tell me something new; decided in my favour. 'She's already bent a teaspoon, Alec.' He opened a drawer in the sideboard and took out what at first appeared to be a silver bracelet; it was one of those long slender spoons they use in those expensive coffee bars where you can never get a decent cup of tea. He gave it to me and I slipped it on my wrist, opening the circle slightly to make it possible. Immediately I was aware of a warm feeling of communion again.

'It's nice, isn't it?' Geoffrey said, proudly. 'I think we could sell these.' You could tell it was another battle he had fought and lost; his eyebrows were full of money again. He said: 'She's as stubborn as her mother. You know what Joyce was like.' It was the first time he had hinted that if I was Morag's father then I must have been fucking Joyce about the same time he was bringing her roses from Kingston. 'Ahem,' he said.

Wherever you find middle-aged and elderly electronics men together you'll hear nostalgic talk about the old days, old technologies, about valves and output transformers and quiescent push-pull; about glowing heaters and coated cathodes and the early plumbing on the first centimetric radar. In essence it's very much like old gardeners talking about cabbage roses or fishermen the pike they cut their teeth on in the days when water was clean. In our world it was miniaturization that brought about the deluge, transistors, printed circuits, the integrated chip that Columbus sighted from the top of his palm tree.

'I can't keep up with it, Alec, and that's the truth. I get all the technical manuscripts vetted. Pye's are good for that. Well, all the manufacturers are. There's always somebody ready to earn a consultancy fee. I suppose you wouldn't be interested? Ragusson pays well.'

I told him no.

'What are you earning then? If you don't mind me asking.'

'About fifteen thousand.'

'Christ,' he said. 'And you don't go to work every day, do you?'

Although editing for a technical publisher, Geoffrey has remained very old-fashioned in his concepts. He talks about 'going to work' and 'gramophone records' and 'wages' as if nothing has happened in the world. He couldn't quite grasp how one operates without a boss or without times to keep to or little offices and little desks. I work through a technical consultancy agency. I am to servo what a brain surgeon is to medicine. Half a dozen companies call on my services.

He said: 'Kids won't work now to get anywhere, Alec. They want it all on a fucking plate. Grants, that's the thing now. They all live on grants while they piss about trying this and trying that. We had to strip to the waist to learn a trade. Look at you, ordinary working-class bod – fifteen thousand a year, work when you like, treat people like Ragusson as if he's shit. Christ, I wish I was you. And yet I've got a daughter who can crack plates and bend spoons over a distance of a hundred miles! I ought to be able to use that, Alec. We want a good agent. I haven't got your initiative, that's the trouble. I reckon you could do anything you wanted. You don't play the clarinet now, do you? Or did I ask?'

I told him I didn't and he seemed relieved.

'Poor old Joyce,' he said then. 'She backed the wrong horse.' To my horror he started to cry. And that's when he said: 'I killed her, you know, Alec.'

It had taken I don't know how long to get the answer to the first question I had asked that evening; the reason I came to Wembley. We sat in prison, two deserted prisoners, one dead, one escaped and no sign of the cavalry, and discussed our crimes; the way you confess your own sins in order to encourage someone else to confess theirs. I didn't tell him everything. For his one dead I had a half a dozen wounded. Maybe half a dozen dead too if you count the abortions. I won't mention who had which and I probably don't know half of them. Morag said afterwards I gave Sandra all the love, devotion and loyalty I'd withheld from other women all through my life. In other words I was an apprentice human being until the Yellow Bird took off from Kennedy.

'Promise me this, Alec. If you go off me don't kid me. Don't waste a hundred years of my life.' You will gather this was not said on the first day; this was after a hot day in a ball-bearing factory in Birmingham. I'm something of a specialist in the noise meter method of feed control. We had called in at David's that night and Caroline had brought her up-to-date on me. Caroline has this thing of innocently telling every girl I take there every foul thing about my past history. Anyway, we came to terms with it. Everything about me that I hated, Sandra hated. It's the strongest bond you can have. Some girls don't mind your faults. Those girls are no good to you.

I didn't tell him everything; I didn't mention Joyce.

'I used to go mad in those days,' Geoffrey said. 'It was partly frustration with my job. Drive suicidally, just to frighten her if she had upset me or if I felt insecure because somebody else had looked at her. The milkman, anybody. We were at the K-garage that evening. Getting petrol. You know, where the M1 starts? We were talking about the college interview. It went well. She talked about Suffolk during the Napoleonic wars. That's where the Flying Fortress is. Nacton, near there . . .'

Difficult to put them down, these incoherent ravings of Geoffrey's. I remember some comic show on television in which a fat chap kept charging up and announcing 'I'm the Kaiser!' This is what I was thinking, sitting there in Moribund Avenue listening to little Laurel delaying the moment of the crash.

What I was wondering was how somebody had got the little Chinese Christmas lanterns to stick up on the ceiling with no visible means of support. There were more puzzles for an engineer. A flight of red and gold butterflies in diagonal flight across the wall and mirror, lots of shiny bright Christmas crackers playing ring o' roses on another wall, balloons everywhere, netted in tinsel, paper pom-poms also on wall and ceiling. Nowhere a sign of anchorage.

'Geoffrey. Just a moment . . .' I told him what was puzzling

me. He was quite pleased that I had noticed it. He was
secretly delighted and proud with every manifestation of his
daughter's (my daughter's our daughter's your daughter's)
para-physical powers.

'She just puts them there,' he said. 'Then she says : stay!
Like that. Stay! And they fucking stay! I mean there's a
fortune in it. And yet she can't get up in the mornings.'

He was full of little passing lines like that which mean
nothing and everything. A whole relationship lies in such little
lines. Geoffrey is the smallest minded man in the world. He's
got a midget inside him. I once saw him spend two hours – I
was not there the whole time – turning 'tea' into 'steak' on a
bill I had paid at Forte's Swiss Cottage; forging himself an
extra two pounds. With such a man the drama of killing his
wife in a jealous rage was not going to be much more than
passing the time. I don't propose to go on with it.

During the quarrel at the filling station Joyce told him that
Morag could do as she damned well pleased with her career
and education. Geoffrey drove off like a maniac and intended
to frighten her. He hit a concrete lamp standard.

'I never got any insurance for that,' he said, bitterly.

Automation has more heart.

In which we talk to ourselves.

You will have noticed, if you are a little more interested than
I was at the time, that never at any stage did Geoffrey
challenge me; on the one hand he joined the general opinion
that I was Morag's father, but on the other he would not
embarrass me with questions. Morag told me later that Joyce
was quite explicit without naming names. Mr X had made her
pregnant, she had tried to get an abortion but had no money,
had appealed desperately to Mr X who, however, by this time
had family troubles of his own and did not reply. Then there
was Mr Y, since it was a simultaneous equation, who was
ready to marry her but she did not love him. Then there was
Geoffrey. Through it all ran dear old Uncle Alec Ranger whom
Joyce would never hear a word against.

'I always knew you were my father,' Morag explained. 'We all knew. It was accepted. Mum didn't want any blame to attach to you. Whenever we heard about you you were full of family problems or work complications, leading a full life, flying to Africa. It was nice. It was as if our family had been specially endowed. Dad kept a scrapbook of you. . . .'

Coming in when I did with everything rhyming and Sandra in Brussels and the world a new empty place, I was a new member; it was like joining my own fan club.

You have to appreciate as well that they all knew each other. Ragusson's Technical Publications and Danny's Wine Bar and even my principal electronics client Webster's were connected by social and parochial veins of friendship. Joan was Arthur's mother, Geoffrey had contrived to get his Wembley neighbours jobs, the way the working classes do cling together pooling their insufficiencies, spreading their miseries across the face of the earth. One integrated transistor-ized chip, big as your thumbnail, would replace an entire red-brick estate in Wembley, wipe out all the sweat and body odours and crushing into the nine-fifteen, the bickering and whining and competing, the copulation and babies and gorging of food, borrowing of lawnmowers.

Who wants membership of such a club? Not your average engineer. They see less than the sowbug of the world around them. To them the miracles of God Scientist are lost in the next news flash.

'Oh yais, I had an uncle like that, Uncle Jake,' Joan recalled on one occasion, after one of Morag's well-known long-distance psycho-kinetics had brought down an expensive and elaborate window display in Lawley's china shop in Golder's Green. 'He used to turn the milk sour.'

Joan would not know, for instance, that selenium, delicate as a leaf, changes its specific resistance according to the light falling upon it. That it brings her her nightly television. Electronics for the million was the original intention of this book but I seem to have got side-tracked. I am beginning to doubt whether I shall find a technical publisher for it. Any-way, there was this Morag club and I was the object of it and

99

the last point I intended to make at this stage is this : Who did the research?

And is Morag's Flying Fortress a musical group?

'Alec! Alec!'

In the cold hard half-light of Wembley Geoffrey came running from his house waving something in front of him. 'Your case!'

'What?' He gave it to me through the car door window.

'Ragusson got it back. I knew he would. Ahem.'

Ahem is right; somebody had carefully re-riveted the handle back on. Somebody had had it a long time and rubbed some leather polish into it. It smelt like a derelict American bomber in my mind. 'Morag gave it a rub up for you,' he admitted. 'It's Sandra's school satchel, isn't it? I expect you're glad to get it back.' Shit. I couldn't talk. Every time I try to be inhuman something like this happens. I drove away crying. Unhuman. She used to put her haggis piece in this case, along with the tiny neat handwritten homework. 'She used to leave it everywhere, Alec,' Janet once told me. 'Then she'd walk miles to get it back. Mr MacPherson got it forer herer out of the harravest money.' Can't you hear the knock on the door, the storm blowing the shutters, and there she stands in her short navy duffle showing her red knees above her wellies, the hood with the poky top pulled down to her lovely eyes. 'Could I just have my wee satchel back, Alec? I'd be much obliged.' You're crying, aren't you? Of course you are. Switch on the windscreen wipers.

Before I reached the end of Moribund Avenue, Morag's Flying Fortress came beaming in to the rescue. No cracked plates this time. A tiny, homing, comforting, radio beam; a high-pitched top-frequency threshold whistle in the head. Any of you who have flown big jets will know what I'm talking about. It's a feeling of being taken care of in the dark. The next thing that happened, minutes later, was this girl crossing the road at the junction of the Avenue with Wembley High Street; which, as you know, is quite brightly lit. She stopped and smiled and waited, the polite manner pedestrians have of not trusting motorists an inch. As I passed her, a foot away, my window open, you remember, I noticed two surprising things about her. One, that she was wearing a T-shirt with a yellow apple on the chest and two – that I knew her. Well. And she knew me.

'Hello, Alec!' she called.

'Hello – er – there!' I called back, with my deadly accuracy. Who is it, quickly, snap snap snap; different environment, different clothes – one of my daughters? Elaine! Elaine Bowen! The office girl from Webster's who had been in love with me since before I ever knew Sandra, who still looks a cheeky twenty-one though must be twenty-eight I should think (she doesn't appeal to me in the least except as a coffee-maker), who even turns up at my night classes at East Finchley and now appears to live (she could be visiting) at least eight miles to the west in wormy Wembley. The whistle in my head had now brought me a friendly face; put her name in the margin. Elaine Bowen: brown hair, freckles, perennial hockey type, warm as toast, sympathetic till it hurts. Two months after Sandra went, when I was at my worst and couldn't go out, she brought some drawings and specifications up to Chalk Farm. When I let her in she stared around for a minute without speaking, then burst into tears. She cried all the afternoon and finally I had to get one of the other girls to come up and take her home in a taxi. Belsen, I am told, has the same effect on people. Next time I saw her she said, in anguish:

'Oh, Alec. How can you stay there by yourself? In that same room? That poor dog, too. Do you think it's fair?'

'You come and live with me, then, Elaine.'

'Yes, I would like to. But you would soon hate me for it . . .'

I looked at her quite a bit after that, and I used to try to fancy her, the way you want to find a good use for something you've got. But I knew her too well, had known her too long; she was like a daughter. But we only knew each other at coffee-break level. I didn't know her surname for a long time – not until she began classes – and I never knew where she lived. She vanished several times, popped up with other firms I visited, was ill for more than a year – I don't know what it was – and she became a friend of Sandra's when they were both on the temp circuit. Now here she was crossing a road in Wembley.

Looking rearwards through the mirror I could see that she had now crossed and was walking, skipping rather, the way I had come, along Moribund Avenue. It was more than likely, I thought, that my homing whistle had just guided me to a few interesting answers. It was much more than likely that Elaine knew Morag, that I had struck another parochial vein and discovered the source of Morag's researches into dear old Uncle Alec Ranger. B-29 'S for Sandra' began to take on a ghostly insubstance. The morbid ramblings of a brain-damaged child – my homing whistle stopped.

'I'm sorry,' I said. 'No, honestly, I really am.' Do you ever get the feeling you've offended somebody? The warmth of her support had gone and I felt chilly; closed the window. As I wound the handle, the only part of the Chevvy not powered, the homing signal returned, weakly. When I replaced my hand on the wheel it vanished. Yes, you have guessed the reason; it was the bracelet. Morag's bent coffee spoon around my right wrist, which I had conveniently forgotten to return to Geoffrey, had been acting as a direction-finding loop aerial to her radiations. The reason the sound had stopped was that I had taken a wrong turning. And she was right – I had. Wembley is one of those places you can't get back from. Not without losing your way. Unless you stick rigidly to the North Circular Road, an abysmal compromise between ring road amateurs and those shrivel-minded jerry-building councils of the thirties, now the longest urban bottleneck in Europe, you are going to come to a series of five-way roundabouts with no signposts to anywhere decent. Willesden, Harlesden, Acton, Kingsbury, all the depressing places nobody wants. It is not generally known unless you happen to have got an 'in' through traffic signals, that some local authorities will not advertise other local authorities by putting their names up on sign posts. Highgate might signpost to Hampstead, for instance, since both places have something of a glamour charisma, but would not mention Tufnell Park or Hornsey or anywhere plebeian. A favourite game is to lead travellers for half the distance then lose them by suddenly removing the name at a vital T-junction. This is why you can't get out of Wembley to any place worth going to; only to other Wembleys. In point of fact this entire enormous red-brick, functional area, dotted with five-way roundabouts and shopping broadways, probably containing a million people, would be ideal for the community negative feed-back treatment. Seal off about six main arteries and it would coexist with itself quite happily. One good solid-state bank in the industrial and commercial computer would more than compensate. Reduce the working week to, say, two days, and such community isolation becomes a real possibility. Feed in such elements as, say, the Royal Family or other national identity coefficients – tours, visits, personal appearances – and the new industrial revolution is almost here. Already you will find such mind-bending security objects as shop names – W. H. Smith, Sainsbury, Boots, Woolworth, Marks and Spencer, Dewhurst, ABC – sprinkled in the broadways in much the same way Piccadilly Circus was nailed on to jungle trees in Burma during the war to give the survivors hope, no matter how stark and unlikely and shatteringly unhomely the surroundings.

Properly organized and with its brain rhythms analysed, simulated and fed back, Wembley could be the country's first hap-hap-happy non-participative consumer cell. The Queen could live at the Stadium, ready for each event. The monarchy has a real and fundamental importance in the new industrial revolution. To replace Queen Elizabeth the Second and Prince Philip with a button would be a mistake.

The personal relic as an aid to extra-sensory perception is well known. To find that I'd got a bent coffee spoon that told me every time I deviated from my route to Chalk Farm was new and exciting. It seems to combine the occult with the practical; this seems typical of Morag and her particular brain deformity. My experiments were interrupted by the police.

'Good evening, sir.'

'Good evening.'

'Is this your car, sir?'

'Yes.'

'Do you mind if I see your driving licence?'

'I haven't got it on me.'

'Insurance certificate?'

'No.'

'I see, sir.'

The policeman now did a short tour of my big car and found that he couldn't get me for tax but he might for tyre-tread; though he had bigger hopes in his mind. He was a bland, sophisticated thirty, cool as a cube and in no hurry. His friend had stayed back in the Jag for a quiet drag; they were taking it in turns tonight. He came back; his number, which I felt I might need, though I was ready to confess to anything short of murder rather than risk an endorsement, was 685. He was a sergeant.

'Do you mind standing out of the car, sir?'

'No. Certainly.' I stood out of the car.

'Do you have to hold on to it, sir?'

'No.'

I stood unaided and without sticks in some dark Willesden Road. He examined me without comment.

'May I ask where you've come from and where you're going?'

'I've come from Wembley and I'm going to Chalk Farm.'

'Chalk Farm. You're driving north to get south?'

'North?'

'You are now between Kingsbury and Edgware.'

'Good lor.'

'We've followed you up and down about four parallel roads, zigzagging from side to side and waving your arms about. Have you been drinking, sir?'

'No.'

'I see. That's inclined to make it worse, sir. In a magistrate's view. Do you always drive like this, sir?'

'No, of course not. I'm an electronic engineer. I was trying out this bracelet. Have a look. Put it on if you like. It's been made by psycho-kinesis. The daughter of a friend of mine has abnormal brain powers. She had a fractured skull in a car accident. Her mother was killed. Anyway she can do this sort of thing, bend metal, crack china and glass, over long distances. She works from a crashed American bomber in Suffolk. That's her sort of psychic HQ. When she presses the bomb release this sort of thing happens. Oddly enough, I noticed tonight it acts as a kind of homing device. I noticed this high-pitched whistle in my head. Take off the bracelet and it's gone. Change direction and it's gone. Every time I wave my arm or zigzag the car it goes sort of bleep-bleep-bleep-bleep-bleep.'

'Can I look inside your boot, sir?'

'Yes, of course.'

'What's all this, then, sir? Women's clothing? Jewellery? Boots, shoes, handbags, umbrellas, dresses, skirts? Are these yours, sir?'

'No, of course not. They belong to my girl-friend, Sandra. She went away to work in Brussels. I heard she was coming back to collect all her things. We lived together. I couldn't bear to get back one day and find them all gone. They're getting a bit mildewy there, I'm afraid. They've been here in the boot over a year now. There's a lot more stuff in the flat, of course. It's a kind of museum. Well, we were getting married until she met this Belgian – '

The sergeant waved me to silence, closed the boot lid, walked a few paces and gave his colleague a whistle. Then he stepped back to me, showed the bracelet. 'This spoon came from Forte's Coffee Shop, Swiss Cottage. Where did you get it?'

'Dick!' The other young copper was now out of the Jag and stalking around the front of my car in a highly excitable state. 'This is it! This is the identical car!'

From the look Dick cast at me you would think my car had been used in a hold-up and a guard had been killed.

'This is the same bloody one. Chev '64.' The young enthusiast, for this I now recognized, thankfully, looked at me. 'Has it got a power hood?'

'Yes.'

'Do you mind opening up the engine? What is it?'

'V8, 6.5 litre, twin carbs, automatic choke, power assisted brakes, automatic gears – '

'What does she do?'

'Sixteen to the gallon.'

'How much oil does she use? Have you had it long? I'm getting one myself. Whizzzzz! Straight up the A12 to Norwich Saturdays! What? Would you mind putting the roof up and down . . . ?'

There is always a slow wind down from police interrogation. A good place for this appreciation of the dubious freedoms is behind the wheel of an American car tacking south through north London, the stereo playing the Grateful Dead, the satchel on your lap full of the only childhood you care about, the enormous boot of your Chevvy packed with the corpus Christi of your solitary love affair. Your bracelet back on your wrist, pulsing you home, a conspiracy and a communion between your deep subconscious and the universe and the abortion that got away.

6

A number of things run into each other here. If I separate them it will be for the sake of clarity. I don't intend to begin to be clear. This is how one gets one's emphases wrong. Who believes in Morag's Flying Fortress? Nobody. Good; nor do I. Not at this half-converted stage of the equation. Who believes that Sandra McPherson will leave her Belgian author and come home to Alec and Moosh? Nobody. Right. Who believes that Ragusson will persuade me to make use of my Continental contacts and secure the para-physical brain bending treatise for his tatty old list? Nobody. Correct. Who is venturing a shrewd guess that Alec is in danger of shacking up with Vicky and starting a new prison? Everybody. Blast.

In the meantime, everybody is asking me what I'm doing for Christmas. 'I'll tell you why that is,' David said. David Ballantine with me in the saloon bar of The Barge at Camden Lock at Sandra-coming-home-time. 'They're all working for the police. They're waiting for you to lead them to where you murdered Sandra and buried her body. It's to do with all her belongings in the boot of your car. We all know that at Christmas you have to be with her. Where you going for Christmas, Alec?' Some of the regulars got in the way of his rhetoric.

'Good evening, Mr Ranger. How's that little doggie, then?'

'Look out. Here come the fuzz,' David said. He had been staring out of the window, hoping my hopes, in spite of his cynicism. Cyril came in, brushing December rain from a black raincoat. He smiled at David, gave me his diagnostic stare.

'Thought you'd be here. Still all right?'

'Fine.'

'I've got something to show you,' he said.

David ordered a complete round of drinks, including Sandra's, which he stood by her empty stool.

'What do you make of this?' Cyril Dyball was showing us a classified ad in *Time Out*.

> Morag's Flying Fortress. Ideal holiday retreat.
> Sleeps five. Sited Suffolk. Offers : Box 259

We stood and drank our drinks and looked at each other. I knew them both well enough to know that I was the one seeing the ad for the first time. Although David had not mentioned it, I was their rendezvous; this is why David had been watching the street. Some telephoning had been going on between Tottenham and Scotland Yard. Cyril's bland Jewish face, round as Mr Jaffa, balding, darkly jowled (wearing a fez you would swear he was in Casablanca), was tilted back, watching me, ready to comment or laugh, waiting to see which way it would take me.

I said : 'Is this a joke?'

'It's genuine,' Cyril said, 'if that's what you mean. I had the box number checked. Somebody called Jock McDonald. He lives in your house. The garden flat.'

'I think I've seen him. A middle-aged Scot. Wears red braces and walks like a gunman. His hands low and stationary.'

'Let's go and shoot him up,' David suggested.

'That's what I thought,' said Cyril.

They were staring at me to see whether I had any secret objection; whether I knew more about the ad than I pretended.

'Who's Morag?' Cyril said.

I told him who Morag is; and who she thinks she is. The detective listened to my explanations as if checking them against a list in his head, then said :

'That's what I understood. That's what David said.'

David said : 'I think it's a load of balls.'

I said : 'So do I.'

Cyril said : 'It sounds like an elaborate con trick, Alec. Except there are too many coincidences. Why should you take your book to a publisher where your old pal works? Why should his daughter turn out to be your daughter? Why is this aeroplane with her name on it, so to speak, being advertised by a man who lives in your house? Where you've been living since long before you encountered Geoffrey whatsit. And if it's a con trick what's the object of it?'

David said: 'Tell Cyril about Ragusson.'

I told Cyril about Ragusson and psycho-kinesis. About Vicky and Tonne, Joan, old Ralph and Arthur and then, as an afterthought, about Elaine Bowen. I didn't mention anything about the whistling bracelet. And there were a number of things they didn't mention. Something had been going on between my best friends. They were not ready to tell me what it was yet. It was connected, I knew instinctively, with David's forthcoming mystery flight at Christmas; and with the fact that Cyril had been out of touch. Probably out of town. Instead of making amusing wisecracks about his police activities, which was usual, embroidering them with what Rose had said and what the kids had said — he put up this image of a policeman with an anti-police family, his only road to promotion being via a nose surgeon — instead of that, he was directing short questions at me. Like this last one before we left the pub:

'When exactly did you last hear from Sandra, Alec?'

They had reason to believe that my Sandra was dead. Their reasons were not very convincing.

Cyril Dyball and his family, Rose his wife, Deborah and Catherine his daughters, live at Temple Fortune near Golders Green, known sometimes as the London ghetto. It is a happy, glossy, shopping and residential boulevard toasting material success. The poor don't live there and millionaires don't live there. People who own shops and restaurants live there, script-writers and television producers live there, the children go to the Henrietta Barnet school in Hampstead Garden Suburb and go riding on the Heath on Sundays. For a policeman to get such a family and enjoy good Jewish cooking in such a place is unusual. Cyril began with a small advertisement in a Brussels newspaper. It coincided with the death of his mother and the break-up of the family home; and also with his first serious promotion to detective-sergeant.

The ad was written in English and he carried a cutting of it inside the deepest recess of his pigskin wallet. He showed it to me on the Trident flight to Brussels on that terrible Friday. It read:

> WANTED English-speaking Belgian girl as au pair in London. Secure home ...

Flying out from Heathrow on that miserable day Cyril gave me some good advice. He told me that Sandra was right; I should not try to intrude into her new freedom.

'Give her a couple of years, Alec. If there is anything of value in your relationship she'll want it. At least she will let you know. Nothing is going to wipe it out. Except maybe you. You could wipe out all the good things she remembers by turning into a neurotic stranger.'

Rose had come to him from Mechelen in much the same way Sandra went to Brussels. Rose had a lot to get away from.

'I think there was an adopted child. At first there were forces trying to get her back to Belgium. Friends, relations — a man. She stayed in Temple Fortune. I didn't pressurize her. Finally we fell in love and got married. Her parents have a farm near Ostend. They are my best friends now. I am going there now for the weekend. Another time, she'll come over with the girls while I'm on long duty. I'm the best fed copper in London. And I'm international. Nobody can call Temple Fortune England. Not in English, anyway. I'll take you where you want to go. Give me that piece of paper. Cheer up, mate. I know where to get a drink. ...'

There was a lot of laughter in the Dyball family. When Cyril took me home after that strange coincidence of sitting next to me on the flight back, Sunday night, after Sandra had brushed me off in that underground dungeon, they took me in and looked after me as if I was a road casualty.

'You are going to eat some food.' This was the first thing Rose said that I remember. A warm, dark, pretty woman; a sexy Jewish mum. With every glance she understands every little lurking problem in your head. The two girls, Catherine fourteen already, pot-resin under her mattress, watching and listening as if I am another lesson in living. They got into my life quickly, meeting me, as a surgeon meets a person for the first time, holding his entrails. That was the night of the rescue, the lifeboat crew meeting each other for the first time: Raymond, David, Janet, Moosh, Cyril, Rose, Catherine and Debby.

But what you are not aware of, after I have engaged your sympathy at a deep and compassionate level, is how much is going on behind the scenes on your behalf. I was not aware that David had sent Caroline to Brussels to talk to Sandra and failed to find her. I was not aware that Cyril had been to Wimbledon to see Isobel and her nuns; that he had been to Altnacealgah-by-Lairg to see the McPhersons. That nobody had seen my Sandra since the day she set off from the Avenue Molière to collect her clothes and possessions from me. I was not aware that Jacques Conte had been to all the places Cyril had been, searching for Sandra McPherson; and that he had finally called at Scotland Yard and mentioned my name.

I was not aware that ever since the morning when everything rhymed, the morning of blessed amnesia, the breeze pressing comfortably chill on my skin, the smell of late chrysanthemums, ever since yesterday's madness had gone, I had been followed.

'What you doing for Christmas, Alec?'

Speaking as an engineer, which is what I am, not a writer, not a private eye, not a killer, a deserted engineer, what the question holds is a template. What I do this Christmas might hold the clue to what I did last Christmas after I'd posted yet another desperate SOS to Brussels containing also a lock of my hair and Moosh's footprint at the top of the paper, in soot.

'Meet me on the beach at Portreath Xmas morning – Alec.'

I didn't expect a reply, you understand. By that time everything was one-way. I was still kicking after the execution like a cockerel with its head off and she was already on to the custard and prunes. Another country, another lover, another car, another set of friends, the Belgian literary set. I still can't imagine what they talked about after orgasm. Whatever held her, it was unlikely she was going to disrupt her set Christmas – you understand I am now back two Christmasses – in order to catch a plane to London and take a long train ride to Redruth in Cornwall and then the little bus that wanders the lanes down to the cove or the double-decker that climbs over the cliffs and drops down to the tiny stagnant harbour on the switch-back road from Camborne.

But I sent the SOS and I loaded up the car, put Moosh aboard and pointed it south-west. As a PS to the SOS I had told her that I was bringing all her belongings. There is something in a Scot that will risk executing her ex-cell-mate for the second time rather than lose five years' hard-earned clobber. This, apparently, is what did the trick.

'Will your young lady be coming, sir?' asked Mrs Bennet's tiny Cornish voice at the far end of the line. Number one harbourside cottages, tap the little door for the widow Bennet. She will have the flat warmed up for you, the sheets aired, a hot-water bottle in a worn knitted cover in the middle of the double bed.

'Oh look! We've got stone steps! I love stone steps!'

Sandra loved stone steps. The house, when we got it, farmhouse, converted watermill, oast house, was going to have steps leading up to an old stable half-door and balcony dotted with geraniums. Not carnations. Cactus, tumbleweed, geranium, flowering cotton-wood. But for now we had a harbourside flat at Portreath, seven pounds for the week out of season. 1969 gave us a hot October. We walked the cliff paths picking wild flowers, awed by the cliff-top defences of Nancecuke germ-warfare establishment. We walked the long coast road around St Ives with the reluctant poodle; crossing little streams running red with tin. We got the late blackberries along the valley road, we shopped in the ubiquitous supermart, we cooked in the small modern kitchen, taking the trouble to put vegetables in the new rack, yet eating with the relish of campers. We bathed with the door open and called to each other the remarkable things of the day. Outside, day and night, the tiny smelly harbour filled and emptied, boatless; out in the bay stood huge Gull rock. Under the cliffs we paddled the rock pools, ran through the surf fully dressed, daring the dog who ran an excited and alarmed parallel course high up on the beach.

In 1970 we did it again and for longer and this time everybody knew us, discreetly, as Mr and Mrs Ranger.

'If you go back on your own you're mad!' cried Elaine Bowen. 'If you go back on your own I shall be very angry, Alec!' This was a girl whose surname I did not yet know. She said I would throw myself off the cliff when Sandra failed to appear. She painted various vivid and believable pictures of me lying crying on the same bed, climbing the same stone steps, doing all the same things; but alone. Except for the ghost.

'Why do you think she won't come?' I asked.

'You know she won't come. If she thought you really intended to drive three hundred miles for nothing she would find some way of letting you know; of stopping you. But she can't communicate with you now. One word from her you would take as encouragement. You would start telephoning her again. You haven't forgotten, have you, Alec? All night long. Waiting for her to pick it up and then hanging up. She doesn't want to start all that again. Don't go, Alec. Please don't go. Or if you go give me the address so that I can come down there. If she's there I won't let you see me. If she's not there, and she won't be, I might save your life. There is somebody else for you, Alec. You are not looking hard enough. Nobody stands a chance.'

I would get all that, just going into the print room and asking her for an ammonia copy. I would leave her crying. She irritated me, but at the same time she was somebody who knew why I had shrunk. I had discovered gold and thrown it away, thinking it was fools' gold. It could not happen again. I have to interrupt the programme for another 'for instance'. It is important that you know that Sandra McPherson is an entirely genuine person. A lot of very nice people I know are not entirely genuine. What they give you is only as much as they've got available. That is to say, not everything. Even for themselves they have not got everything of themselves.

QED: In a pub or restaurant Sandra would not spare glances for strangers. Would not act a part, wondering how we looked to other people. Would not raise her voice to give strangers an intriguing sample of her intellectual or outrageous conversation. Would not bully me or treat me in some quite alien way to give listeners or an audience a false impression. Would not have a secret train of thought involving herself with some promising man at the end of the bar and apologizing to him for her present companion. In a pub Sandra would be unaware of her own entrance.

Now I want you to start your own list in the margin of your friends who are unaware of their own entrance into a pub or restaurant. I have my own list of twenty-four people, made since Sandra left me; only one is unaware of his own entrances. Not one woman is unaware. Sandra lives for the person she is with and for the moment she is in. All this I threw away, thinking it was nothing. Believing it was ordinary. No Belgian novelist is going to recognize these qualities in a Scottish girl. She is purrafect. And all she wants from life are stone steps and a few tubs of geraniums. No button will ever replace Sandra McPherson; you cannot automate the optimum person. You can only automate for inefficiencies. Sandra, with her earnest boy's stare, would do everything to absolute perfection. If she didn't she would worry about it; then do it again.

'Alec.' she said one day, out of something, possibly, that Françoise Sagan had put into the novel she was reading. 'Do you think I criticize people too much? I think I criticize people when they're not around. I do talk about some people. Say nasty things, sometimes. Or criticize them just by implication. Just by mentioning something they might have said or done. I know I do. I do. Alec. I'll have to watch it.'

Listen. Jacques. Listen. That's a wonderful girl you've got there. Purrafect. And sometimes she would cry because nothing was perfect any more. The cell grew smaller and Amnesty International were unaware.

'I can't even play the violin,' she used to say, when she had the miseries, squatting on her mat, looking through the bars at the hard world. 'It's all right for you, Alec. You get some satisfaction. You're changing things. You're right in the front. I'd like to get involved in something useful. I've been thinking of the Common Market. Going into Europe. Last time I went home I thought about it. All the girls who were going to be teachers are teachers. All the rest are mothers, pushing prams. Nobody's moved, Alec! I could drift back to Lairg. I've got to do something, Alec.'

Sandra McPherson, standing on her own two feet in Europe, refusing to hear my cries. What are you doing for Christmas, Sandra? Well, I don't know what she did. I never got any farther than Stonehenge. I should never have tried to pass Stonehenge by myself. There was something about those stone teeth in the stoneless countryside that touched something quite primitive in her. We always stopped and just sat and looked at them. When it got dark I was still sitting there. Out of her school satchel I had taken the note she left me the first time I spent a night away from home; trying to be unfaithful.

Dear Alec,
(Monday morning): I love you and I've missed you like hell. I'll never leave you if this is what it's like being apart. I slept all right with Little Dog close to my back all night – I don't think either of us budged. I got up okay and have just put some coffee on. I'll take Moosh out before I go, cos I've got lots of time.

LOVE AND CHEEPERS
Sandra XXX (8.01 a.m.)

'Hulloo there, Captain! Mr Ranger. Are you all right?'

A vaguely familiar face, wicked but kind, beetling grey eyebrows and short grey hair, a stocky Scot; Jock McDonald. He was seriously concerned and also very cold; he had been sitting in his Land-Rover without a heater, watching me. 'Morag told me you were driving this way. I promised to keep an eye out. She was very worried about you.'

'Who's Morag?' You understand I had never heard of Morag at that time; Geoffrey was still in the past and in the future.

'Or was it Elaine? Aye, Elaine Bowen. You remember it was through her you got your flat. I told her about it.'

'Oh, Elaine!'

'I'm the Scottie fellow that puts all the bottles by the dust-bins. In the garden flat.'

'Yes, of course, I'm sorry. No. I was driving to Cornwall but now I'm not so sure.'

I don't know whether you appreciate the impact of such a meeting. It may sound casual and in fact he tried to make it sound casual, but it was not casual. The whole thing was mounted like a commando operation; I'm not at all sure there were not troops in the back of his Land-Rover. Here was a man I'd hardly seen or been aware of before, dressed in some antique remnants of a USAAF squadron leader's uniform, decorated with various yellow flowers straight from dope corner at Haight and Ashbury and wearing also a peaked denim cap with a reinforced steel bullet-proof crown and with a gun holster tucked in his Sam Browne and no doubt live grenades inside the bulge of his tunic pouch, trying to sound casual.

He leaned his elbow in and stuck his Scottish face within inches of mine, grim but compassionate. 'Don't go to Portreath, Alec. You're making a dangerous mistake. Your lassie will not be there. Better if you fly to Brussels and confront her and that wee Belgian prick. Shoot him. Make your decision. But don't go to Portreath hunting ghosts, laddie. Sandra will not be there. You can't go back. A woman knows this. And so do you. You've sat here staring at these bloody rocks for three hours! Your dog is dead in the back seat. Follow me into Salisbury and we'll find it a wee dram o' whisky. Don't go to Portreath for Christmas. . . .'

Although it was not a casual meeting, about seventy miles from London on the old A303, neither was it as portentous or dramatic as it may sound. The Scotsman can make a weather report sound like the millennium, can give any awful warning a feeling of authenticity, such is his affinity with the past and with the dead; given a certain dry and thespian comicality a character like Jock McDonald could top the bill at the Glasgow Empire. But he was not comic to me. Nothing was comic to me at that time, 22 December 1972, less than six months after my woman had broken out.

Ordinary living takes ordinary nerve and I was a mental statistic. Waiting for the bus that never came, cleaning the saucepans with brick dust. Being an Aunt Ruth, the sad and the lonely and the lost.

Do you know Salisbury at all? And if so do you know the White Lion hotel; very traditional with a white front looking on to narrow shopping streets, boxes of geraniums on the window-sills, a square opening the size of a stage-coach, the driver with a top hat, leading into a cobbled courtyard and a big glass entrance. It seems now like one of our places, Sandra's and mine, though I am not certain that we stayed there overnight more than once, breaking our journey to the West Country. There was a night we wandered around the cathedral close and a night we had dinner upstairs at a venison house, overlooking the ancient crumbling stone fountain-house, or whatever that monument is. Sandra was not certain whether she liked the rich, over-garnished meat, or whether she would have known it was not beef, had she not been told. But it was in the quiet hotel bar-lounge that something happened – in my mind, that is – to bring about the state of calm that made it possible for me to begin this technical report.

Sandra was always happiest when we had booked into a hotel. All associations have been left behind, you are on a desert island and you belong only to each other. You are loving each other, you are doing things you would not normally do, workaday; too many of the days of the year go past in a dull routine clockwork manner. You are in prison and you are not aware of it. The porridge seems normal, the evenings seem like freedom, the nights like passion or rest; you are doing nothing special, looking forward to nothing special, because you do not care for it just now. You are too free to have to give thought to freedom. But now you have run away from all that. Ahead lies dinner and here comes the aperitif brought, chest high, by a Chinese waiter. We could have a Chinese waiter in Chalk Farm; it just never occurs to you. You have bathed and dressed with some care, you are feeling extremely solicitous of each other's well-being. Doing strange things has made you slightly strangers and politeness and romance begins to overgrow familiar clearings, hard-trodden.

'Do you feel all right, Alec?'

'Yes, thank you.'

'The drive was not too much for you?'

'I enjoyed it.'

'So did I . . .'

I love you. I love you too. I love you more . . . Do you begin to recognize the symptoms? If this is love, what is it we have at home all the time? At ground level? And how long has your partner been quietly sawing away at the bars? How far has she got with her tunnel? The dog perhaps can tell you. When she lies with one ear half-alert, when all apparently is quiet and peaceful, then somebody is digging a tunnel. Switch on the tape I have in the museum and you will hear Sandra ask me if I would like some coffee. She asks me six times in ten minutes and there is no reply except the rustle of pages. And then, heartbreaking to hear now, she breaks into a little Highland song of her childhood.

The moment that hit me so poignantly then, because it was a duplicate moment, while listening to Jock McDonald my rescuer in that same bar and perhaps at the same table, but maybe a year later, maybe two years later, was the moment when the waiter brought his tray, chest-high, walking with vigour and style, it being the first order of his evening. Nothing happened; we took our drinks, I a dry martini, Jock a whisky. But what came back to me was this. Just as our Chinese waiter came across the quiet carpeted floor amid all the old brown woodwork, our dog, Poodle, Moosh, who had been lying at peace with the world, both ears unalerted, under a table or chair, suddenly remarked the coming of the aperitif with a loud solitary yap:

'Al'k!'

The Chinese waiter's hands went up in the sky in fright, the tray of drinks flew over his head, his eyes held the look of a man who is facing some horror worse than death. Crash! came everything down on the floor. Moosh, who having passed her remark had settled down again, now raised her face in alarm and pressed herself deeper into the shadows. Sandra and I apologized to the waiter, insisted on paying for the lost drinks, and did not laugh to fulfilment until he had gone to fetch some more. It was the most profoundly comic happening and one that could not satisfactorily be recounted; everything lay in that Oriental's face.

'She loved you, Alec, no doot aboot that! But she wanted a new life with a different future – Germany, Heidelberg, the Swiss mountains, Scandinavia. She's a European, Alec. . . .'

But the moment of the bark came back to me and I knew he was talking rubbish; Sandra belongs to me for ever and every few hours, days, weeks anyway, she must discover it anew. So that was the something, followed by a number of other things, that led finally to my state of calm. I was going to get her back in my own scientific, skilled, engineering fashion. I was fighting a Belgian prick, an artist, writer, a man without mathematics. A savage, Robinson Crusoe might say. Sandra is capable of bad female judgements.

'She had an affair with Michael Fash, the debt-collector Jew in Islington,' Jock McDonald told me. 'I hope you can bear me telling you about it now, Alec. Oh, she was in love with him at the time. He promised her a directorship in order to get her knickers off. No English girl would have believed him! You may remember. I don't know how much you knew at the time. She would come down to me when you were away or asleep and tell me all the troubles. Well, for God's sake, Fash was one of those odious tin tycoons, keeping his staff at each other's throats with false promises and false confidences. Keep an eye on the company secretary, Sandra – I'm thinking of giving you his job. Don't let Sandra see too much, George – I have a feeling she's after your job. In the meantime he is screwing her after hours and complaining about his wife, bragging about his killer dogs, mourning his dying father. He's a truly lovely person! she used to tell me.'

'But that's what she said about Jacques Conte!'

'Well, exactly. And that's what she'll say again about you. When there's no one else left. You've got a brain, Alec. If you want her back, use it. Don't go keeping tryst with the past on Cornish beaches. Wait, bide your time, be strong, be rich, be powerful – be home and waiting. It's infallible! For a Scottie lass it's infallible! If it's going to help at all, have somebody take care of the Belgian. But don't martyr him. Let something quite undignified happen to him. Give me time and I shall think of a number of things.' Murder, you felt, would be the least of these things, if it were to help a friend.

Counting my stores and my blessings, as Robinson Crusoe did, hoarding goats and coconuts and bent nails, frightened of the unknown savage who had already kidnapped half my couple, this Scotsman, Jock McDonald, came as robust reassurance, aggressive as an armed squad and ready for duty. This is before I was cast up on the island where everything rhymes, you understand, or discovered the footprints.

'You can go back home for Christmas, Captain,' Jock told me that night when we had eaten dinner at the White Lion in Salisbury, 'or you can fly to Jersey and spend Christmas with Barbara.' He seemed to know everything about my life, my women, my past. Barbara had a shop in St Helier before she went into business in Nassau. 'Mary would welcome you in Exeter so long as you don't stay too long.' He was right, she would. We would catch up on the not very exciting news about all our married daughters; some write to me and some to her, neither of us write back. 'Or you're welcome to follow me, Alec. I'm spending Christmas in the country with friends. You remember the old crew. I have to warn you it's a bit damp these days. The B-29 was not designed as a hunting lodge, you may remember, Captain.'

I remembered nothing. I considered he was crazy. I did not know the old crew at all, I did not know why he kept calling me captain or how he knew so much about me. On the other hand he was one of those familiar, affectionate people; it would hurt them to confess you do not know them as well as they know you. Also, I was not very well. Jock McDonald was part of the fever I was going through at that time. I did not see him or hear his name again until a year later, nearly Christmas again, when my detective friend Cyril Dyball showed me the ad in *Time Out*.

Morag's Flying Fortress. Ideal holiday retreat . . .

So we walked up the street together, the three of us, three men, hurrying along the damp pavement of Chalk Farm Road, past the entrance to the locks, under the railway bridge, dodging across the one-way bleed-off road, dancing into each other's way and changing places, coats and jackets flapping open, intent and excited like three cowboys who have just heard there's been a shooting at the livery stables. I remember thinking that men do not often walk together on the streets like this any more; now the fuel was running out. Unless something happened it was the beginning of the end of the fully automated man.

Our ages were roughly these : myself fifty-six since July, Cyril, my Jewish detective friend from Temple Fortune, forty-three, David Ballantine about thirty-four. And it was three days to Christmas 1973. I can't bear textbooks where the facts are not crystal clear the whole of the time. We are moving through another equation now to a rather incredible quotient. I am wearing the golden apple on my T-shirt; perhaps the freakiest of three rather straight men. The air of Camden is still chill on my skin and the fine hair riffles my scalp; every passing smell I am aware of, conscious of the thoughts of other people and carrying Geoffrey, Morag, Ragusson, all the other inhabitants of the island quite sharply in my memory bank. Vicky I was not prepared for. I am never prepared for Vicky, those nipples pushing into my destiny. Flesh and scent and yield yield yield, pretty, vacuous, sensuous eyes, copied from the stag magazines, thighs open, inferior, slave, mind-emptying embrace, you come into her mouth like conversation, no stature lost.

She had heard me at the door and was lying on her front on the purple bedspread on Sandra's museum bed, her face lying sideways on her hands, under her long hair, her lips parted, tears gleaming on her cheeks, her elbows spread like butterfly wings, one breast naked and in view, one knee raised high, pulling a little white pinafore dress above her crutch. I closed the door and put the catch on and undid my trousers as I went to the bed.

Her dog, the Great Dane, was lying on the floor with its arms folded, watching; Moosh was under the bed, just her nose out, her beady eyes fixed resentfully on the intruder.

'Alec!'

'Don't move,' I told her.

I fucked her up one leg of her panties without giving her any special consideration, knowing that Cyril and David were in the flat below and would be up at any moment.

'Oh, darling,' she murmured, quite a bit too late. We did that thing of going through short romantic preliminaries after the event, to leaven the incident and remove it from the animals' domain. Then she said, as soon as she decently could: 'I've bin kicked out. Them fucking bleeders got a petition up. They said I'm a pro!'

I said: 'You'll have to get kicked back, Vicky. I've got some friends coming in.'

'Don't take it out. Not for a minute. I've got some news for you. Your girl's come back. Sandra. She's downstairs.'

I took it out.

There was a knock at the door. When I got to it, dressing myself, Vicky scrambling around behind me, the dogs growling, David was already walking away. 'Come down, Alec. There's something you've got to see. Hurry up.' He was gone round the bend of the stairs. Vicky joined me at the door, whispering:

'She let me in with her own key.'

'What did she say?'

'She asked me if I was your girl-friend.'

'What did you tell her?'

'I said I was just visiting.'

I looked at her, standing there tear-streaked, trying to wipe my semen off her crutch with her knickers. She said: 'You're not angry, are you?'

How could you be angry; she'd put on a great show just to make sure the news didn't spoil the evening. As I went out she said: 'Can I have a bath?'

It was not the way I had visualized reunion with my Scottie lass. A marathon opera would not encompass the million reunions I had dreamed and planned. But at its most sensitive, the fingers of the heart touching all at once, the reunion was by the rocky pool at Portreath, sunlit, tideless, enduring. I love you fuck love woof woof love you love woof fuck fuck fuck kiss hold me lock lock lock together unto the grave.

'Come in, Alec!'

Jock's door stood open. Cyril and David appeared to be alone, examining the flat minutely, like the scene of the crime. It was a pigsty. The kitchen, narrow, entered directly from the outside door, was grubby beyond belief; the cheaply carpeted floor had dirt grimed into it like boot-polish, together with embedded milk-bottle tops and onion skins. Somebody had made a start, a brave start, on the filthy sink and draining boards and a year's washing-up. The smell was Jeyes fluid desperately applied for survival. Milk bottles had various quantities of yellowing cheese and curd stuck to the glass, smelling like cat's shit. Incongrously the smell of cooking came from the oven and Cyril pointed to the automatic time-setter.

'Somebody expects to be back at eleven o'clock tonight.'

David said: 'Has he got a girl-friend?'

'I don't know. I never see him.'

Cyril said: 'He's gone away. Been gone about a month, I should think. Somebody's moved in. Recently. Half the flat is clean and she's working this way.'

David said: 'Who could it be.'

They looked at each other as they had been looking at each other all evening. They thought they knew what I didn't. They'd seen the BEA Brussels labels on the luggage in the bedroom. I said:

'It's Sandra.'

Their surprise was gratifying. Cyril said: 'How long have you known?'

'About five minutes.' My wet foreskin was sticking painfully to my leg; Cyril wouldn't know anything about foreskins. 'Vicky's upstairs. Sandra let her in.'

David said: 'How does Vicky know Sandra?'

I said: 'She sleeps in the museum. There's at least two hundred pictures.'

'Come and look at this then, Captain,' Cyril said. He was determined to surprise me. And he did. Over the white marble mantelpiece in the big living room of Jock's garden flat was a three-foot-wide framed photograph of an American B–29 bomber on a wartime airfield, the captain and his crew standing dwarfed by the undercarriage in a long football team kind of line, all furred and helmeted and uniformed up. The caption said:

B–29 Flying Fortress at Great Gransden October 1944. Skipper Alec Ranger and his crew.
From left to right: Gunners Vincent T. Smedder Junr, Rodney Bekker, Charles H. Lee, Ross Woods, Richard Jeskins, Al Mathers. Navigator Jock McDonald, Flight Lieutenant Alec Ranger, 2nd Officer John Ragusson, Bomb and Missiles, Geoffrey Neasden and Jean-Claude Conte, Radio Officer Irwin Cloot. The pigeon basket contains Betty Grable and Dorothy Lamour. This plane, the last of the old Forts with many Superfort modifications, was shot down during a mass raid on Dusseldörf.

It took me a long time to read it all, trying to assimilate the facts offered and failing; aware that I was being closely observed by my cowboy friends. The killing at the livery stables turned out to be nobody less than the sheriff. Scotland Yard had a special diagnostic scrutiny waiting for me; Cyril, I mean. He spoke first:

'Anybody you know?'

'I would like a magnifying glass,' I requested. For the second time, if you remember; the first time Geoffrey was showing me his family album. Cyril sorted out a folding glass from his pocket Sherlock Holmes outfit and I applied it to Alec Ranger on the distant, thirty-year-younger airfield photograph.

David said: 'Is it you?'

'No.' I stepped back, cleaned the glass on my sleeve. 'It's a clever fake, David.' They both stared at me as if I had just confirmed long-suspected lunacy. I said: 'Well, that's what you

want me to say, isn't it?' They were quite hurt. Cyril said:
'I'd just like the truth, Alec.'

This was the truth: 'The face could be mine. It's about
twenty-six years old, has a RAF moustache. The only thing
against it is, I was never in the Air Force. Royal or American.'

Cyril said quietly. 'The records say you were, Alec. So does
your family. So do your old friends. So do your old flying
colleagues. So does everybody who knew you before you came
back from Danzig in 1971.'

'So does Sandra,' David added, as if throwing brandy on a
Christmas pudding.

I said: 'When did you talk to Sandra?'

'Before she left you,' David said. And he said, reluctantly
and with some sympathy, it seemed to me: 'After you lost your
memory, became automated. After somebody replaced you
with a button, Alec. . . .'

You must have had this situation. Somebody you see nearly
every day starts talking as if he's been sitting in the desert
thinking about you for forty days and forty nights. What I said
was this, just to shut them up and mention the realities: 'Did
you break in here?'

'The door was locked,' Detective-Superintendent Cyril
Dyball said. 'I can't resist locked doors. We're going to have to
level with him, David. Alec, I've got something to confess.
You're not just my friend – you're a job. When I sat next to
you on the Trident coming back from Brussels that Sunday,
it was no accident. The captain put me there. Everybody was
nervous about you from the time you went through Customs.
A few weeks before the Brussels Trident had crashed at Staines,
everybody dead. The week before that somebody less demented
than you tried to open the door at 20 000 feet above Ostend.'

'I wasn't demented!'

'You were demented. Here he comes! everybody was saying.
Everybody watching you. Padding around that bloody great
concourse at Brussels airport, hot, no drinks, queues for everything, all the planes late, a shirt hanging out of your case, the
toes out of your running shoes – you weren't even dressed!'

David said: 'I don't understand how Sandra could let you

out like that, pushing you off alone with your life in pieces, specially on a Sunday, of course you were demented. You were still demented when you got back here. Ray turned the gas off at the main before he went. That's your own son. You must have been demented. You raped Janet. Demented or desperate. I mean Belsize is bursting with decent arse.'

'And who's that tart upstairs?' Cyril suddenly asked.

'Vicky's not a tart. She's a ballerina.'

'Get rid of her,' David said. 'Caroline thinks your taste has fallen to pieces lately. What's Sandra going to think?'

'I don't give a shit what Sandra thinks! Sandra's been fucking Belgians for the past eighteen months.'

'There's water coming through the ceiling,' Cyril Dyball said, observantly.

There was water coming through the ceiling.

7

The water was coming down through the electric-light fittings.
This is a highly dangerous situation. But never mind that; it
rang more bells for me than anything on the island. Than anything that had happened or been said, that is, since everything
rhymed; since I had come ashore. Not only was Vicky's per-
fumed bathwater pouring down out of the electric light socket,
but you could tell, from the floor beneath, from the cracked
damp ring in the ceiling, that it had happened many times
before and Jock McDonald, being Jock, had done fuck all
aboot it.

No memory hammer, not even that photo blow-up of the old
Fort, hit me so hard as this dim, tatty, grotty reminder of our
pissed slut of a navigator.

'Jock! Are you awake? Where the fucking hell are we? Is
that Dusseldörf? Will somebody kick that Caledonian shit!'

The voices crackle through the inter-com and through the
wood and the creaking trees and through my brain-washed
head. We flew our missions with the Yanks at Great Gransden,
loaded with liquor and tobacco and with any screaming bit of
uniformed arse we could grab aboard at take-off. We all had
Joyce and Alice and a beautiful American Air Force girl
sergeant whose name I now forget, while flying in formation
on target course over Germany and occupied Europe.

With the water coming down and the picture on the wall
and Sandra's luggage in the bedroom and the smell of a
casserole in the flat and the automatic timer ticking away
like a bomb towards eleven-fifteen, pub-closing zero, David
Ballantine took hold of my shoulders, as he had done at night
school if you remember when I was chatting to Jeni Thirshall,

and he did the same thing, reading my face like a newspaper, and he said the same thing: 'You're over it, Alec! Don't tell me you don't remember now! All better! You're over it, Skipper Ranger!'

'I am not over it!' I told him, spitting the words into his face. 'I refuse to be over it!'

David had had the hardest time of all with me. He had known me the longest. Sandra had had a hard time and Morag had had a hard time and my ex-wives and children and relations and friends had written me off as somebody else, but David had stuck with me all through. He hugged me now, as was his wont, and he said: 'And Sandra's home! Here! She'll be coming through that door in a couple of hours!' It had worried the life out of him that he had sent her away; he felt that he had destroyed my life.

Cyril tried to remain as calm as a policeman but he was smiling, his face in the lamplight like a happily mouldy orange, blue around the chin. 'We'd better go up and stop this water – '

'Don't switch off!' I knocked his arm away from the wall switch; he was about to switch off. 'The spark may ionize the water and blow the main fuses.'

'Aye aye, sir,' said David. He has always been proud of my scientific knowledge and writes AMIEE after my name, even on birthday cards. David is very non-technical. I have seen him try to open a sash-cord window outwards.

Here then was another eruption. They were getting bigger and louder and more insistent and more relevant. To be truthful they were nothing. They were the breeze growing a little stronger, the fine hairs riffling the scalp a little more, the smell of winter now cold and wet and beautifully alive with promise right up there in the nostrils. To a robot the merest whisper of a chill breeze sentient against your tin must be good. A turn for the better.

Vicky's bath had brought the neighbours out. This was a Christmas so economically depressed that an overflowing bath was like a carnival. The bells were ringing and the doors getting knocked and people shouting when we came up from the garden flat; water was jetting down from the bath overflow and cascading on to an asbestos flat roof, forcing passing pedestrians into the traffic of Belsize Lane, splashing into parked cars and somebody's kitchen window. Above the sound of the water and the protest and alarm came Vicky's loud singing from the open bathroom window above. You should know that I was not aware of her condition when I burst in and fucked her. She had arrived to give me news of her pregnancy, that mixed state of mind, half accusation, half excitement, another half defence and reasons why it could be nobody else. She had met Sandra, which had reminded her that I was in love with somebody else. She had drunk half a bottle of gin before I got there and the rest of the bottle in the hot bath since. She was singing the yellow taxi song, about knocking down Paradise and building a parking lot.

'Do you know who it is?' This was a neighbour, Phillip something – famous name on the doorplate, one of the names of the century. I said I didn't know who it was singing. 'She's ruined my bloody dinner. Soapy water in every bloody saucepan.'

'She's in your flat, Mr Ranger,' a little old lady said. I don't know her name even after eight years; she brings round all her chicken giblets for Moosh, green and putrid with age. I have to hide them at the bottom of the dustbin under Jock's bottles.

'Oh, is she?' I said. 'I'll go up.'

Cyril said : 'It's his mother.'

David screaming with laughter; all of us going in, laughing and giggling like schoolboys. We enjoy ourselves away from women, away from Caroline and Rose and Sandra. Married men ought to ride about in motor-bike gangs sometimes.

There was water all over the living-room floor, soaking the carpet; all my records and books untidily chucked behind the settee out of sight, all wet no doubt. Shit. I banged on the bathroom, but Vicky's singing went on. Cyril banged, David banged, I kicked. The dogs line up behind us, Vicky's Great Dane suddenly getting agitated. It started barking a deep Great Dane bark. 'Al'k ! Al'k !' Moosh joined in. The bathroom door opened and Vicky's wet scarlet sweating gin-soaked naked body appeared, all tits.

'Did you say something?' she asked.

'You're causing an affray!' Cyril Dyball said. He put out a hand to close the door a little for politeness' sake, but the huge dog mistook his intention and pounced on Cyril's back, got his big teeth stuck into the policeman's shoulder.

'Get him off!' Cyril cried, and something in Hebrew like fuck or God.

'Dicky! Off! Off!' Vicky came out and hauled the monster away. Its great Stonehenge molars had gone through Cyril's shiny black raincoat, which appeared to be bleeding. That was as much as we could see until he stripped to the waist. Cyril was really frightened.

'He's broken the skin a bit,' he said, in that falsely casual way when you're trying to be nonchalant about impending death. Being a policeman must have made being brave more important. 'I don't suppose it's much. It's not turning blue, is it?' He started putting his clothes on. 'I'll just pop up to the Royal Free and get an injection. I distrust animal bites,' he added, apologetically to the girl.

Vicky said: 'He never poisons people. Sit down and give him your paw, darling. Oh, look at his big eyes. He's saying sorry.'

Cyril was already out of the door. I decided to go with him; he looked as if he might faint. David couldn't take his eyes off naked wet Vicky. 'I'll stay here. That's right. I'll be mopping up.' He has a sexless marriage on his hands, remember. I knew who he was going to mop up.

We couldn't get a taxi, then we got one.

From what just happened you may not be aware of my mental and physical state. There was a good deal of hysterical over-excitement between us that had nothing to do with bath-water and was rooted firmly in the equation. Morag's magic carpet had now got wings and a crew. The prisoner that escaped was back and banging drums. I had checked her luggage, the same big check case she had taken out of Customs at Nassau airport, the same case she had packed for Brussels, almost unnoticed. There was something slightly wrong about the casserole; it did not have her smell. But David knew and Cyril knew that the casserole and the flood and the crowd and pulling down Paradise was only the dancing tail of a strange enormous kite in my guts, pushing out the mathematics; that the sound of the cavalry bugle was in Chalk Farm, that Sandra McPherson was home and that I was almost home, in my mind, nearly the flyer again, Skipper Alec Ranger. Dying of tetanus was uppermost in Cyril's mind now, the last bit of coloured paper on the kite tail, but Sandra coming in with her little musical third of a whistle and into my arms was uppermost beyond dying.

'You know what Rose says?' We sat facing each other in the taxi, 7432, brown trim, black driver, because detectives have to see if they're being followed. 'She says she would give the last few minutes of her life in exchange for the few minutes of your reunion with your girl. Just to see it, she means.'

'A few minutes?' It didn't seem very important.

'It's important when you're dying. Everybody standing round. Trying to make it last.' He was clutching his shoulder now, seeing it, his own death scene, about midnight in Temple Fortune. He said : 'Put your hand on my jaw. Tell me what it feels like when I grit my teeth. It goes in and out, doesn't it.' He had leaned forward and I tried it.

'Everybody's jaw goes in and out when they grit their teeth.'

He was convinced he'd got lock-jaw. When he was a sergeant, he said, he'd had to take a man to hospital who had been badly bitten by a kitten. 'He couldn't open his teeth finally.'

'If you're so worried about tetanus why don't you have the injections?'

'I've had the injections.'

'So why worry now?'

'I don't know !'

Then what he did was, he sat and laughed at me, his Jewish, Mr Jaffa, mouldy orange face beaming and gleaming in lights from the economy-lit Haverstock Hill. I was laughing too, the kite soaring higher and higher. She was probably in the George. No, she was probably – no, I know where she was, she was with old Ruth having one of her little boozy reunions in the Swiss Cottage, all girls together, Janet, Eileen, Valerie, Lee Girl come back to my place, sleep on the floor, oh, we're sleeping at Jock's, you should see the dirt –

'You're going to be all right, Alec.' Cyril put his hand on my leg, gave it a reassuring pat. This is really all it was about; a policeman shouldn't get so involved. He sat watching me, quite fondly, like a craftsman watching his job. And what I already knew, I knew again. I was his job. He didn't deny it. If you want to get the absolute truth out of somebody, interrogate them in out-patients when they think they're dying and they can smell all the accessories.

'Are you on duty now, Cyril?'

'Yes.'

'Were you on duty when we met going to Brussels?'

'Yes.'

'Are you on duty whenever you're with me?'

'Yes.'

'Are you on duty when I'm eating with Rose and the girls?'

'Yes.'

'Are they on duty?'

'No. Well, no. Where's that bloody doctor. Why don't I get attention? I'm the police.'

'There's your answer. How long have you been working on me, Superintendent?'

He didn't want to tell me any more.

'Is you face turning blue? I think your face is turning blue. Can't you answer? How's your jaw? Your teeth are jammed together, aren't they?' He laughed and I laughed and a number of accident cases looked up from *Punch*.

He said: 'You've been my job ever since you put that text-book into Ragusson. *Automatic Control in Industrial Processes*. Before that you were somebody else's job – MI6 for want of a better word. Only they didn't know who you were. Does the name Solzhenitsyn mean anything to you?'

'Yes. I worked for him in Danzig. He's a Russian neurologist.'

Cyril sighed. 'You're the only person in the world who would give me an answer like that, Alec.'

'I don't understand.'

'Of course you don't. You're an engineer. I doubt if you ever read a book that didn't have mathematics in it. Anything cultural in your robot mind was wiped out in Danzig. That's why Sandra went.'

'Are you trying to tell me I've been brain-washed?'

'Yes, Alec.'

'Have I lost my memory?'

'Part of it. A chunk of it.'

'Mr Dyball?' A pretty sister, this one, but badly timed. 'Will you come this way, please?' He didn't go for a second or two; instead he said:

'What does prison mean to you, Alec?'

'Marriage,' I said. 'Shacksville.'

'That's right,' he said. 'It's an obsession. Have you ever been to prison?'

'No.'

The sister, beautiful NW3 *mädchen* in uniform, was taking him away as he made my unknown past public domain. 'Yes, you have. Two years in a cage, Alec.'

'I didn't kill anybody, did I?'

'That's what we don't know yet,' he said.

Moosh had escaped.

'David went out and left the door open,' Vicky said. 'Well, I pushed him out. Your friends aren't half forward.' I'm sure there was a lot more to be said about that but I was in a panic about the dog. She's a nuisance, you have to feed her and give her drinkies every time you have a cup of tea, take her walkies at three in the morning – but then, suddenly, she's out there in the dark and can only say Al'k.

'I'll look for her,' Cyril said. 'You go down and wait for Sandra.'

'No, I'll look for her. You get dressed,' I told Vicky. She had a baby-doll nightie on now; I didn't know where she'd got it from until I went to look under the bed, just to see if Moosh was hiding from the Great Dane; nothing could hide under the bed, it was stacked with suitcases and hold-alls and bundles of clothing, a guitar, record player and a whole balloonage of kitchen utensils, kettles, frying pans, saucepans, tied together with string.

'I'm only staying the night,' Vicky explained.

'How did you get it here?'

'John dropped me off in his shooting brake.'

Ragusson had dumped her on me with all her worldly possessions. I told Vicky that she had to fuck off.

'He's right,' Cyril said. The way your friends kowtow when they've offended you. 'I'll run you home.'

'You haven't got your car,' I told him.

'I'll call up a buddy. Police car.'

'I haven't got a home,' Vicky said. 'I've been kicked out.'

'The Samaritans have got a doss-house at Euston – I'll take you there.'

'With George?' George is the Great Dane.

'I don't know about George,' Cyril admitted.

'That poodle's going to get run over just before Sandra gets home,' I pointed out.

'You'd better come home with me,' Cyril said, as doubtful about Vicky's tits as the dog's teeth in a place like Temple Fortune.

I said: 'You can't do that, Cyril.'

'Look, mate, it's the lesser of two evils. If your reunion's buggered up I can never face my family again – go on, find that bloody dog. Hurry up, Vicky.'

'Shall I get dressed?' Vicky said. And she caught my arm before I'd got away: 'Do you know what you're doing for Christmas yet, Alec?'

I went out without answering her and then I went back. For a robot I was getting a lot of funny human feelings. One of them was that this poor bloody girl alone in London devoted her life to that huge dog, sold herself for him.

'I'll ring you at Cyril's tomorrow,' I told her.

She's got a nice smile.

But I really went back for the bracelet. They watched me get Sandra's school satchel from under my pillow, take out the bent spoon and put it on my wrist. You see, they were in the club. They know as much as you and I do.

'Good luck, Alec,' Cyril said.

'John's looking for you,' Vicky told me, as an afterthought. She had taken off her nightie and was struggling into her clothes. 'That's why he give me a lift. You might know. He's been ringing you all day. Here, where you been? Nobody could find you.'

'I go to work,' I said. Then, testing something I said to Cyril: 'Tell her where I've been, Superintendent.'

'Hospital,' he said. 'Hammersmith kidney unit.'

I said: 'You had a long wait.'

He laughed. 'Not me. There's six of us at least. Shift work, you know.'

Vicky said, her face tragic with concern: 'You haven't got bad kidneys, have you? Is it catching?'

And automation for blood scrubbers is part of my job; traffic signals for home kidney units, electronic writing for the deaf, emergency communications, fail-safe alarms.

'Alec ...' I was really going this time, Morag's beam whistling in my head; Vicky was full of last things. 'Can I ask you something personal? Do you think you'll still love her?'

Always and always and always, said my clockwork heart.

Ordinary living takes ordinary nerve.

I followed the beam through Chalk Farm, knowing roughly the route, lamp-post, gateway, tree; our prison exercise yard before the great escape, following Moosh north towards England's Lane, west towards Swiss Cottage, trying a few wrong turnings with an engineer's curiosity, just to hear the signal die, then getting back on course.

'Is that the North Sea down there, Jock?'

'Where, Cap'n?'

'Underneath us, man!'

'Is that *underneath*? I been lookin' at that! It's a great wee lot o' wa'er is that. ...'

You may wonder why Morag's para-physical jewellery should first of all beam me home from Wembley to Chalk

Farm, now steer me unerringly as a guided missile after a lost dog. If you wonder things like that then extra-sensory perception is not a subject that is likely to play a very big part in your life. It is Morag's brain damage that is giving her the power that some possess naturally and some after psycho-surgery and some after Dr Solzhenitsyn's drug cycles at the Danzig neurological institute.

Now that the equation is simplifying, obscure abstracts converting into something like common sense, phasal lubricants cancelling out, now that we can contain the entire perimeter on one blackboard, as it were, now that my mind is a good deal clearer than the first morning when everything rhymed, this walk through Chalk Farm in the dark, using a bent spoon like a water-divining rod, searching for a poodle, hoping to meet a girl, seems to me now, at the time of writing the report, to be the very first time that I began to realize that I must have been off my head ever since —

Since when? Since Sandra escaped from our little jail? Or since that weekend in Brussels when she didn't love me any more, loved Jacques Conte instead? Or since Danzig? The returning memory, or, more accurately, the returning mind, plays peculiar, subliminal tricks. I began to get some very funny feelings as I walked the dark streets, the villas moving back as I passed like icebergs, some lit with Christmas trees and coloured lights and tinsel, others dark and gone away. I whistled and clapped and called occasionally, but the signal in my head was getting louder and I felt sure that I was fully automated, that manuals were unnecessary. A jetliner passed over, a deep roar in the clouds, a Boeing 747 on its glide path into Heathrow, also locked on a runway beam. I remembered the Boeing high above the Delaware valley, Sandra's face against the porthole, her fluttered smile, I love you, I love you, I love you more; I remembered sitting behind the controls of the Fort, coming in low over a dark shoreline, a woman clinging to me, hysterically; Grace, yes Grace, the blonde American WAAF whipped out of the mad drunken party at Joyce's house and across to Dusseldörf.

'Alec! Are we going to crash?'

'Not if I can clear the trees. Jock, where are we?'

'Does it matter, Captain?'

'Belgium,' somebody said. I think it was Irwin's last word. This is why we believed it.

Double image now, the kind you get on your television screen, a scan harmonic in the time base. One picture has two heads against the flight-deck windscreen, Geoffrey and I looking down at trees two hundred feet below and coming up. The other picture has our heads on the Poly roof, looking down across Islington. The beam in my head cut out and I was back in Chalk Farm. The audio had been replaced by visuals and I was bang on target.

The girl with the dog in her arms, six lamps away and coming nearer.

Doh, lah!

Listen! That's her little whistle. That's Sandra's magical, musical third! Doh, lah! You do it. Do it in the margin. Doh, lah! Sing her name on the same notes:

'San-dra!'

Listen to the real Scottish answer as she stops her clip-clop walk:

'Is it yew, Al'k?'

Ah, that's where Moosh gets her 'Al'k' from.

'Is it yew, Sandra?'

'No, it's not – it's Morag!'

The stems of darkness between the white villas were like tree trunks holding up a vast black canopy of sky reflecting a smudgy orange blossom from the main bus routes. I could smell bluebells. She came close to me, her dark eyes like knots in a pale wood, anxiously on my face; a girl with a familiar kindly face, a screw of black hair in the back of her coat collar, a brown woollen tammy ringed with green and a whiskered mole by the corner of her mouth. I knew her as I knew my job; she was in the print room at Elliot's and was in charge of the technical library at BICC, at their Bloomsbury Street offices and in my instrumentation class at East Finchley she sat right at the front. I had last seen her crossing the road in Wembley, if you remember, when I was on my way back from

Geoffrey's with Sandra's school satchel and the bent homing spoon.

'You're Elaine. Elaine Bowen.'

'Not at all!' she said, in outraged Glaswegian. 'Can't you tell from my accent, Al'k? I'm Morag. I'm your own true-blooded bairn.'

Another jet whined its heavy whine on the gradients of the night air, an eleven hundred with faulty exhaust straightened Belsize with the unerring accuracy of ten pints in the Belsize Tavern, his hub cap clipped somebody's bumper, flew past our heads and into a garden; Moosh barked once and Morag put her down. She then reached forward and slipped both hands ungloved around my neck unscarved, massaging gently and with love, speaking softly. 'You're one of my uncles, Alec skipper, and you might have been one of my skulls.' The robot heart softened and a tear sprang from some tin gland.

I said: 'Where's Sandra now?'

Morag kissed me on the mouth. It was like shutting me up; as if I had been obsessed for too long, possessed for too long and she had at last discovered the secret of exorcism. Considering how long I had known her, the kiss was alarming, the fingers of the heart touching all at once, the tide shifting in the tideless pool. I kissed her and kissed her and held her, clinging together, weeping with the need, the dog barking urgently around our feet, wanting to come up and share it, up to human height in the hard world, the misery I mean and the tears because it's not the prisoner you love at all, but the prison.

8

What is never made clear about people who lose their memories or have their minds washed clean or have extraneous matter superimposed, is this : how does the person feel if the truth returns? For my part, speaking as an engineer, which is what I am, always, even making love, the things that came back to me meant very little. They are not a part of what I am trying to set down here in this report. The flower is spectacular but only the root matters; there will be other flowers. It is not what happens in Chalk Farm or Brussels, but between your deep subconscious and the universe. Sandra McPherson had come back to me and I had not recognized her. The drums and the bugles and the thunder of the cavalry were all in my prisoner's soul.

'You met her twice at the dustbins and once you left her standing at the bus stop in Chalk Farm Road.' Morag was not reproaching me, but bringing me up to date.

'But she's had her nose altered.'

Morag said nothing; which left the altered nose as a reflection on the depth of my feelings. She turned her head sideways on the pillow, Sandra's pillow used only once since she went and that was to prop up Vicky's delightful arse. Janet, being Sandra's best friend, had insisted on doing without. Morag had turned her head simply to flutter her eyelashes, as Sandra does, and say :

'The noo !'

Which is a sad kind of nostalgic piss-taking that you get between good friends and good lovers and nobody else in the hard world. Lying on our backs, my daughter and I, our naked legs linked, I told her how I had first found her footprints, about the morning when everything rhymed. She smiled her slow smile as if seeing the whole island on the bedroom ceiling.

'That was me, Alec. Sending you love.'

I don't know what she was like before the car crash, but I'm sure that Morag Neasden is one of those people that brain damage suits. She has a slow, deliberate way with her, as if finishing a mouthful of food before speaking; and you will not hurry her or interject until it is accomplished. Having expressed one thought you will know if there is more to follow because she is nodding her head slightly to maintain interest, as though agreeing with herself. It is altogether an attractive habit. It gives to her soft, slow grey eyes and parted lips an air of pondering beauty, an inner wisdom and satisfaction parting the fog of complexity; the old, remembered personality shines through the brain lesions for a moment on equal terms with the hard world. And when she yields her body it is utterly and completely, as if to the surgeon.

The telephone made a noise sometime during sleep and we untwined, the ivy from the apple. It was David's mother.

'I began to wonder if you were there, luv. Have you seen David? He an't got home all night. Caroline's having a fit. I don't know why. They sleep on the same honeymoon bed wi' a bolster down t'middle. Wouldn't suit me. Any road, I keep smelling petrol and death and 'elicopters! He's not wi' you, is he?'

I told her that David had been with Cyril and me most of the previous evening and roughly what time Vicky kicked him out. I could tell from Morag's back that she knew something that I didn't.

'That's that detective, in't it? She's already rung him. He's a funny one, an't he? Coming round asking your friends all those questions about your past. I wouldn't trust him an inch, Alec. Scotland Yard's never even 'eard of 'im. There's no Superintendent Dyball here, madam, they said. Luckily he left her his private number in case she wanted him in a hurry. I don't know what they're expecting you to do. I think he's a special agent and so does Mrs Willis. That's my friend. Here, is it true you got brain-washed by the Russians when you were delivering summat? You ought to take it to court. Do you think he's got an 'elicopter? Special agents have 'elicopters, don't they? I don't know why but I keep thinking about 'elicopters. If you see David tell 'im to ring 'ome, Alec, there's a luv. Ta-ra — 'ere! Have you got your new girl-friend there? I can feel the vibrations. She's one of us, she is, a white witch. What did I tell you? See round corners, that one. Is she nice, Alec?'

'She's loovely, Mrs Ballantine!' I pulled back Morag's head on the pillow and kissed her hair into the receiver.

'Eee! I 'eard that!' Molly exclaimed. 'You make me feel right restless. Ta-ra, luv.'

'Ta-ra,' said I.

Morag remained back in my arms, watching the museum. All that she knew remained unspoken. In her back and the torque of hair at the nape of her neck. The brain-damaged are masters of the time-slip and communicate chiefly by feeling; and then only the important things. I felt sure that David had received a call from Scotland and had found Sandra with the girls at the Swiss Cottage pub and had probably taken her out to the airport. Morag had come back to see me and to pick up any replies to Jock's ad in *Time Out*. He was down at Nacton tarting up the B-29 and she would probably join him for Christmas. I was now beginning to realize that the dead and the living, her friends in the country and the crew skeletons, the Home Guards and their families, those of us who murdered them and our families, and our descendants and forebears, were all on the same magic carpet, the same desert island, their prisons our prisons.

'Ta-ra!' cried Morag.

'Ta-ra,' said I.

Don't be late, mind how you go, take care, see you tonight, all the affectionate idiots across England parting for the day, for it's early yet, the sun in the air rather than in the sky, everything rhyming at Chalk Farm tube, for it's secretary time; Morag turning to wave, holding her little case, full of all the letters from people who want a little bomber of their own down in Suffolk or somewhere.

'Take care, Alec!'

'You take care!'

Pretty girls in their boy-friends' golden apple T-shirts, worn denim jackets and tight flared jeans. *Mind the doors. . . .*

Back at Special Branch meanwhile :

'Alec?'

'Who's that?'

'Ahem – '

'Hello, Geoffrey. You're early out of bed. Where are you speaking from? What are all those voices?'

'Is Morag there, Alec?'

'She's gone to work. At least, I suppose she's gone to work. She doesn't say much, does she? I just walked her to the station and gave Moosh her morning pee. Lovely day!'

'I wouldn't know. We've been up all night – all right, I'll ask him in a minute – ' this was his voice aside '– Questions questions questions. Still, I'm glad you and Morag got together at last. You've got a lot in common.' He hurried on, as if I might detect the criticism in this remark : 'What are you doing for Christmas, Alec?'

'Who else is there?' I asked.

I heard his voice from the cupped receiver : 'Alec won't tell me. If he wouldn't tell Sandra and he didn't tell Vicky and David and the Superintendent can't find out – what?' 'I'll talk to him,' somebody said. It was John Ragusson the Viking publisher.

'Ranger? I've been looking for you. I want you to go to Brussels for me and talk to Solzhenitsyn – '

'Don't say that for Christ's sake – ' came a voice.

'Fuck off, I know what I am doing. Ranger? Did you know that Jacques Conte is dead? Murdered? Just the way you planned it – '

'Give me that phone, you Norwegian cunt – '

There was what appeared to be a fight for the telephone that sounded like unskilled washing-up and then silence; a middle-class secretary bird then spoke.

'Skipper Ranger? I have Group Captain Lancelot Porker on the line for you.'

Suddenly I was talking to Piggy Porker of Special Branch. This is the kind of thing I have always wanted to do. But now I was doing it I felt foolish. I was sure that in the mix-up of photos from their man at Danzig they had got hold of the wrong person. I resolved next time I was in Shaftesbury Avenue I would call in Selmer's and see if I could play the clarinet. If you remember Geoffrey keeps asking me if I still play the clarinet. Either I am two people or somebody else.

'Put him on,' I said.

'A very good morning, Skipper!' sang an avuncular gin-bubbled public-school voice. 'You don't know me but I know you. Superintendent Dyball and I work together. One can't say more over the open telephone. I take it you're alone? Good. Now I don't want to impose on your valuable time, Skipper, but we would be delighted if you could call in and see us today. As soon as possible, that is. Clear a few things up. This morning for preference, about ten. It gives you an hour. We're at the top of the BBC London Radio building on the N for north, got it? side of Hanover Square, W1. Pull your right ear as you come through reception then straight up in the lift. Is that clear, Skipper? Can do?'

'No.'

'You can bring your little doggie, of course.'

My brain may have been bent a little by Solzhenitsyn but I still know when I'm being treated like a lunatic or imbecile child. I told him I couldn't make it and that I wouldn't have a free day until early in the New Year. He sent the tanks in immediately and sounded much less like a commercial for Benson and Hedges and more like somebody a down-to-earth Jewish copper like Cyril might call 'sir'.

'I don't think you realize the urgency, Mr Ranger. This concerns the safety of the realm. I'll have you picked up in half an hour.'

I told him that I'd be gone. I heard him say, crossly: 'See what you can do with him.' Cyril came on.

'Hello, mate,' said Cyril.

'Hello, Cyril,' said I.

'Did you have a good night, Alec? David tells me you got the wrong girl.'

I said: 'Is David there? Tell him to ring Caroline or his mum.'

'Listen, Alec. We've got to check you out. My boss thinks you've been programmed.'

'To do what?'

'We don't know yet.'

'What makes him think that?'

'I've been talking to Vicky, David's been talking to Sandra, your electro-encephalogram shows signs of negative feed-back.'

'Where did you get that?' The ten-channel brain recording signed by Solzhenitsyn as a souvenir from Danzig hangs in its stainless-steel frame on the multi-vibrator rack in the bedroom.

'Morag just brought it in,' Cyril said, shamelessly. 'How soon can you get here, Alec?'

I told him something more important had come up – work. But I got off the line without tellng him where.

Something quite serious had come up in the morning mail which put all Special Branch frivolities out of my mind; the letter was from chief physicist Claud Harding at the Forest Research labs in Bucks.

Dear Ranger:
Hope this won't muck up your Christmas shopping. Regret to say the moisture-in-timber instrument TFH 587 has developed what appears to be a leakage fault in the core electrode (yes, again!) and the present cycle of tests will be vitiated unless you can ride to the rescue.

This was a pilot kiln-drying process, yet another 'instant seasoning' idea aimed at hungry building programmes. It was being done in a very wet barn by the river at Marlow. What we needed was an idea for preserving at least a million megohms of insulation across the electrodes under these conditions. At saturation point moisture-in-timber measurement is simple but at the dry end of the scale there are too many variables including the weather. Most of you will know this.

The letter had already spent three days among the Christmas mail; I telephoned Harding and arranged to meet him for lunch at the George by Marlow Bridge. There were spares and bits and pieces, measuring equipment – not forgetting the old-fashioned bunsen and a test tube for drying out shavings – from the manufacturers at Park Royal, then quite a long drive up the A41 and across the Chilterns to the Thames.

I felt very sad on this drive because it was Christmas and Sandra was now in Scotland. The letter I secretly longed for is this one that I carry next to my tin heart. She wrote it the first time she went home by herself, when she loved me, loved me, loved me more.

Dear Alec,

I love you.

It was super to talk to you today, because I wasn't even sure you'd be there after getting no reply last night at 12.00. I got a BBC2 set from the shop and had perfect reception going, and all the family watching out for you. [I appeared on the *Money Programme* that week, 'People versus Buttons'] I was disappointed tho' & doubly so when I found you not in, tho' I thought perhaps you'd gone to David's to watch yourself. [I had] Still, I'm glad you're so pleased with it & expect we'll see it together if there's a repeat one day. I'm sorry Wee Jim was being such a pest in the phone box !

Drina and Robert dropped Janet & me off at the Welcome Inn tonight & we had a few drinks there. Donald joined us after about an hour, so we got back all right. [This in case I should think a man took her home.]

Yesterday I bumped into Nan, Maggie's sister, at the shops, and she said that Maggie would be coming to Lairg last night, so Donald took me there. It was super to see her & she raved about my coat. Pat, one of her flatmates, was there too and she sez (sais) I can have her bed for the weekend. Nan drove them back to Glasgow and I went along for the ride. I shall go mad stuck here much longer without you. In the pub tonight there was a little black poodle & a white one, & I felt nostalgic for our pesky little barking dog [Moosh]. I miss her too.

Well, I've just had some Ovaltine and toast with Janet & it seems to be bedtime. I haven't slept much since I've been here & I had a sad dream last sight. I was just realizing it was over & reached out to cuddle you & of course you weren't there. When I arrived I kept addressing my father as Alec : you see I don't miss you only in bed, tho' I can't wait to get back to our bed. So, I suppose I'd better bathe my bottom & scrub my teeth & try and get some sleep. I'll ring tomorrow from Maggie's (before you get this letter in fact) : I'll have a good weekend, as far as circumstances and conscience allow & look forward to seeing you. You can see I'm missing you tonight.

Do your best workwise Alec, & love me as best you can : I'm only a mixed up kid after all. I'm sending you a Scottie £1 note which should amuse Michael [bartender] at the Barge. It is currency, honest.

Good night my old man ! I want to cuddle you and give you lots of cheepers, but until then think of me and miss me.

All my love,
Sandra

PS Don't stay [indecipherable word] up working all the weekend. Have a drink out at least, but no dollies please. Love, XXX.

Most of the brackets are mine except when she repeats the word 'sais'. This is an in-joke. When repeating somebody's conversation, particularly somebody outrageous, she would use the word 'sais' instead of 'quote'. When she stopped doing this about Soapy Joe, the Islington debt-collector Michael Fash, was when she stopped holding him off on the office sofa after hours. Even so, she never ever, even after my well-known personality change, took my brain rhythms to MI6.

Let's take a short break here.

I am falling into the trap of writing like a novelist. Dr Patrick English (Stoke Mandeville, Cell Barnes, Bristol Neurological Institute) asked me to write this report clearly, carefully and factually. The temptation, always, is to create narrative suspense. So far as I know during the time of the rhyming and the breeze, the soul emerging from its metal cocoon, there was never any burning anxiety on anyone's part on the island to know what was coming next. Except, that is, what I was doing for Christmas.

'I believe I may be able to shed some light on that,' Claude Harding said, carefully. Like most scientists Claude is always very cautious about committing himself. He once told me that human life was based on two things, the tangential and the integral calculus. It was after the last day of the scientific instrument exhibition at Earls Court and I think he was a bit cut. We were now sitting over mutton dumplings at the George. In quiet moments between the traffic over Marlow Bridge and the ever-flooding weir beyond the churchyard, he filled me in with a number of things still missing in my head. Harding has that half-timbered look you find in Bucks; very English, medium built, nothing over-done, a strong face and weathered skin, always a pipe, of course, though with one or two extravagant concessions to science and research in his clothing – his top hankie looked like a pair of knickers, for instance. We're inclined to hang on to student gags when the corpus of one's career – unlike the doctor, say, or lawyer – is electronic rather than human. One knows more robots than people. Claude has been with Forest Research at Princes Risborough for more than thirty years. Middle Bucks is full of hotels like the George, the dining rooms attracting serious men in suits and ties, the slim waitress about sixty every time she turned round.

Claude now said, between forkfuls of haricot beans, watching my face as if to register its effect : 'People who don't know what they're doing for Christmas may be suffering from the Gdansk effect.' You got the feeling that 'effect' takes a capital 'E', as part of a disease.

I said : 'Are you talking about the Danzig Neurological Institute?'

He said : 'Yes, I am, Alec.'

Harding would have said nothing else, I'm sure, without invitation or encouragement from me.

— I said : 'What is the Gdansk effect?'

He said : 'Mind blotting by negative feed-back of the brain rhythms.'

I asked him what was its principal use and he did not at once reply, devoting himself to the excellent Marlow dumpling. Then he gave me a shrewd look.

'Tell me something, Ranger.' This use of my surname indicated a shift to the professional friendship of our calling. My heart lightened. Ever since everything rhymed I had needed another engineer to confide in. He said : 'Is this conversation being bugged?'

'Only on my wire recorder,' I told him.

'I don't object,' he said. 'But you must change my name in your treatise. Family reasons. My son is a quite well-known poet. It should be sufficient to alter a syllable.'

'Of course. Harding — is that all right?'

He waved his fork to indicate its unimportance and then said : 'Does the name Jacques Conte mean anything to you?'

You read about people choking but usually it's to indicate that they have been startled while eating. I choked. I got over it without any help, disguising my retching noises with a cough as you do and murmuring sorry, but Harding, being a scientist and untuned to dramatic emotions, went on :

'His father flew with De Gaulle. Jean-Claude Conte. He was killed in bombers, I believe.' Quite suddenly my brain hurt and it must have showed this time, for he leaned across with some concern : 'Are you all right, Ranger?'

'He was my flight engineer on the B–29!'

Harding did not find this at all astonishing; nor would he had I mentioned the extraordinary coincidence of Sandra meeting and falling in love with his son thirty years later in Brussels.

'Well, the father, Albert Conte, that is Jean-Claude's father, Jacques' grandfather, was part of the French end of our pre-war dirigible programme. A gasbag *entente* rather like this Concorde project that's going on now. Albert died in the R101 crash in France. Or was it the R34? Anyway Jacques

148

Conte was murdered yesterday in Belgium — I don't know whether you've seen the paper? He was in the middle of exposing the Gdansk effect.'

'I thought he wrote fiction?'

Harding said, soberly: 'A lot of people would like to consider it so, Ranger. You should talk to my friend Otto Sturm.'

I know Otto Sturm. How do I know Otto Sturm?

'I think you know him,' Harding said. 'He knows you. You worked together.'

'Siemens? Frankfurt?'

'No.'

'Phillips at Eindhoven?'

'No.'

'Not Grundig?'

'Were you at Grundig? No, not Grundig. I didn't say in Europe, did I?'

These little guessing games are precious, aren't they; it gives you both a chance to gallop knowledgeably round your own field. 'What made me think it was on the Continent. His name, I expect. Otto Sturm. It certainly rings a bell. Where is he working now? Same place?'

Harding shook his head, his mouth full of dumpling, turned it into a sign to the waitress to refill the water jug. Engineers seldom drink on the job. Then he said:

'Otto works at Koblenz. The NATO weapons research lab.'

'They were in the news recently. Weren't they in the news recently? I've got an electronic counter there, measuring shell velocity.'

'Precisely — sorry' — Harding spat gravy everywhere — 'that's how it all came out. There was a car crash, quite accidental, near Mechelen on the Antwerp to Brussels road. Well that was the subject of Conte's piece in the *Sunday Times*. The Russians have used the Gdansk effect to infiltrate every top secret establishment — according to Otto Sturm. Otto was over here when it all blew up. We had a good old laugh. NATO secrets all over the road. Well, that's what you get when people don't know what they're doing for Christmas.' He picked a back tooth with his tongue for a moment, reflectively, then added : 'According to Otto, that is, and Jacques Conte. And now Conte's dead. His car crash was no accident. They're looking for a red-headed Englishman.'

There's only one red-headed Englishman on the island. David Ballantine. *Have you seen David? He an't been home all night* . . . That mysterious flight he was due to make at Christmas to an unknown destination. Molly's funny feelings, forebodings, death even (Conte's death?), the smell of petrol (car crash) her head full of helicopters. Then Ragusson's straightforward indictment : *Did you know that Jacques Conte is dead? Murdered? Just the way you planned it* . . . It is quite typical that when searching desperately for some connection, some code word that might explain everything, you remember something rather unimportant.

'Great Gransden,' I said to Harding. 'That's where I knew Otto Sturm. During the war.'

'That's perfectly correct,' he said, and called for the bill. The old lady with the young girl's body came up with the bill, which she had been fidgeting with for some time, waiting for us to stop talking and go. But it was all part of the pleasure of her day with very little else, one would suppose, to go home to. 'Did you enjoy it, sir?' she asked Harding and Harding said : 'Delicious, Mary!' And to me she smiled and said : 'We haven't seen much of you, lately. Keeping well, I hope?'

Voices and faces from beyond the abyss; people who could explain anything of my life which they thought might be unclear. Characters in a C. P. Snow political novel, the only man whose fiction I enjoy, those austere bystanders, as agreeably uninvolved as the wallpaper in any house of horrors. These are the people I have been meeting on the island where everything rhymes.

When we left the George to return to the kiln-drying barn I discovered that I had been followed from London in the best MI6 tradition. Daniel Tonne, most unluckily for him as a trained agent, was coming from the public loo to his car and

I caught him halfway and gave him a hail; he had probably been breaking his neck to pee for the past hour, wondering if he could last out and had failed. He pretended not to recognize me and got into a grey Citroen ambulance; in it were two thick-set gentlemen who, I would imagine, were good at mugging people in the streets – I could almost smell the oranges.

'Who was that?' Harding asked, politely.

Inside the barn I added to what I had already told Harding about the general concern as to what I was doing for Christmas.

'Well it sounds very much to me as if you are suffering from the Gdansk effect and that Christmas is your slot.'

'But it's years since I was there.'

'And were they interested in your last Christmas?'

'No.' Then I thought for a moment more; 'Yes!' People don't follow you down to Stonehenge unless they're interested; Morag and Jock were part of the conspiracy. Cyril was following me to Brussels. The whole Special Branch operation began long before I felt a chill breeze on my skin and my fine hairs rippling on my scalp.

'Do you know what I'm beginning to believe, Ranger?'

'Tell me.'

He went on with his work for a moment; letting the new revelation mature into logic. We are about the same age, Harding and I; speak the same language, breathe a common ambience, political, scientific, human – English. I watched him take notes from the recorder chart. The moisture content was stabilizing now, the surface readings two per cent lower than the core; this is partly a temperature error, as you know, the core remaining hotter and the iron-wire compensation circuit inclined to lag through the wood's low specific resistance and even lower specific thermal capacity (I am talking here of our ubiquitous Scottish pine). He switched on more lights and the afternoon outside the open door of the barn seemed suddenly darker. Traffic across the river was whining up through the Berkshire woods, some with sidelights already gleaming.

Lighting his pipe again, Claude Harding now rejoined me

at the electrode end of the kiln, where the armoured cables came out of the sixty-foot-long iron coffin and the high-impedance insulation meter wavered on the seventy megohm mark; this was our main anxiety this afternoon and so far it seemed to be holding up. I had fitted new highly polymerized electrodes, shellacked and baked to withstand boiling water at any of the pressures we were likely to deal with; I had also fitted new rubber washers and a desiccator in the junction box connecting the electrodes to the recorder. Never forget, those of you who are still student/apprentices that the development engineer faces problems unknown in production. In a pilot system such as this the components, which will finally have all the headaches moulded out of them (together with the leakages), are often quite crudely fabricated. There is no money for tooling until a system has been proved.

'May I speak freely, Ranger?'

'Yes indeed.'

'First of all,' Harding said, 'why do you call Gdansk by its old German name – Danzig?'

'It was most famous as a free port in the Polish Corridor – Hitler's bone of contention. One of his most publicized territorial claims.'

'But the first time you went there it was known as Gdansk? Pride of the Baltic, chief of the three Polish ports – Gdansk, Gdynia and Sopot. Trojmiasto as they call them – rather like our Cinque Ports. It's difficult to see how you could work in a great scientific centre like Gdansk and still think of it as Danzig. How many national institutions are there in Gdansk? Eleven?'

'Seven,' I told him. 'Forty-three research institutes and units – including the university. Ten agencies of the Polish Academy of Science.'

'And who did you deal with at the Gdansk Neurological Institute?' Harding asked me, in the smooth, trick question manner of academics.

'Solzhenitsyn. Dr Solzhenitsyn. He signed my electro-encephalogram for me. A sort of personal testimony to my brain normality.'

'Solzhenitsyn,' Harding said. Then: 'And did you make another chart before you left?'

'No.'

'That's a pity, Ranger. Had you done so you might have discovered that your brain rhythms had suffered the Gdansk effect. The Russians are inclined to sign their crimes against freedom with the names of their dissenting poets. Solzhenitsyn – your man, Alec – was a fake.'

It was a symptom of my recovery that Harding was telling me nothing that I was not already half aware of. Heartbreak and love administered like a push in the psyche and a kick up the arse had already put you in control; yesterday's madness had gone. I said:

'You're talking about negative feed-back.'

'And what is the effect, precisely?'

I said: 'Reduced amplitude in the alpha rhythm and an odd kind of envelope modulation of the beta rhythm. The sort of thing you get in radio transmission, modulating a carrier wave with sound. Except that in the brain, the fundamental rhythm is the low-frequency component and the modulation is centimetric – that's a radar frequency.'

'Quite. That's why the American CIA call it Bats. Combined with a drug cycle they can blot out a part of what's in the mind and replace it with a programme of their own. According to Jacques Conte a number of assassinations and terrorist atrocities have been carried out by walking computers. The Kennedy assassination, for instance.'

'I can't believe that.'

'Conte's dead now so one can't check his sources. According to Conte, among Lee Oswald's souvenirs of Moscow – you remember he had been to Moscow? – was an electro-encephalogram signed by a Professor Tolstoy. Another fake. There is also the hypothesis – was it Lee Oswald who came back?'

'So you think that I've been programmed?'

'More than that, old chap. I may be wrong, of course. But I believe that it was you who put Jacques Conte on to it. Did you have a girl-friend with a name beginning with S?'

'Sandra. Why?'

You will understand that engineers discuss only important things, never private affairs. I had known Claude Harding for ten years but only just learned that he had a son. Now I told him about Sandra and Conte; it obviously informed his present knowledge and he was delighted. Everything I thought I knew about my Scottie lass was quite wrong. She did not go to Brussels and fall in love with a Belgian writer; she went downstairs to the garden flat and cried her solitary confinement to Jock McDonald. We were in the same prison, but my mind had left. This is when it started.

'You got to get away, lassie! Come back when he's better. We'll keep you in touch. Me and Morag. I've got a good buddy in Brussels. The son of one of our old crew-mates on the B–29. You must have heard Alec talk about Froggy . . . ?'

But of course! He was one of them! My good friends! Lover my foot; he was presented to me as a lover so that I would not pursue her. He was Froggy's boy. I never thought of Froggy as Jean-Claude Conte. Froggy was Froggy. The greatest flight engineer a pilot could wish for; now just a cracked skull that won't hold flowers. His son Jacques Conte had been a fully qualified member of the island.

'He was always an impressive science fiction writer,' Harding said. 'It was not until the April demos in Paris that he cut his teeth. 1968 I'm talking about, when the police fought the students in St Michel as if they were fighting tanks. I happened to be there. You knew that whatever came out of United Europe there would be a united police force. That the Common Market was going to be a fascist bloc, a bigger threat to Russia than NATO ever was. So far as individual freedom is concerned I don't think there's anything to choose between them. Russia with her population farming, putting the people out to graze, government by the élite – '

I had to stop him; my skin was creeping with offence. 'Not true. Push-button government, Harding. Science is God, nobody doubts that. The most sophisticated automation is only nature accurately applied. It is not a natural law that every individual born must spend his life working. . . .'

As I went on I had the strangest feeling of double image again, as though my voice was echoing with another voice in another place, a classroom perhaps, where everybody was wearing a set of head electrodes, all wired to the same electro-encephalograph. Harding was there as well, tapping his pipe out on the kiln, watching me, rather than looking at me.

'. . . Solar energy and undersea gas and oil can release mankind to the work or pleasures he prefers or it can make more millionaires. Automation of routine tasks can cause happiness or unemployment – it's up to us to decide.'

'The élite, you mean?' said Harding.

'What?'

He laughed. 'I wanted to trigger you off and I did.' I recalled Geoffrey laughing after he had tricked me into an outburst in defence of my textbook. That's a weakness and I shall have to watch it. He said: 'You're an élitist, Ranger.'

'I am an engineer!'

'You're an automationist, Ranger.'

'I am an automation engineer!'

He seemed to be speaking very quietly or else I was shouting; the barn was warm and there was a slight hiss of escaping steam, the bubbling of the electric furnace pipes under the floor. Harding said, quietly:

'The automationist is not simply an engineer. He is a political animal, a fanatic, Ranger.'

'*I am an engineer!*'

I wanted to kill him. I wanted to kill him!

Harding went on sucking his pipe, looking up at the megohmeter which he now tapped to see if the needle was sticking, but only as an absent-minded aside.

I desperately wanted to change the subject but could only get back to the same subject. I said: 'What about Conte and this girl S?'

Harding said, 'I wish you'd read the article. She had been living in London with a man who didn't know what he was doing for Christmas.'

'I don't understand you.'

Harding said: 'Well, this is how he put it. This is what

gave him the clue. The girl was a friend of a friend. She had been living with this engineer. His name was R. You know how careful they are about libel, Ranger. Anyway this man, we'll say it was you, had suffered a personality change while working with the Russians at Gdansk. Let's say it was Solzhenitsyn. Now, when somebody has part of their memory blocked out and the rest is intact, you are not going to realize it immediately. Only when you strike the part that's missing.'

'Christmas,' said I.

'Precisely,' said Harding. 'Perfectly logical if you work it out. If you programme somebody without their knowledge they cannot fill the same slot twice. They put that future point in time, call it T_1, into a subconscious filing system.'

'Into an equation,' I said.

'If you like, yes. The result is that you don't double-book. Lee Oswald did not know that he was going to shoot President Kennedy in Dallas on 22 November 1963 – but on the other hand he did not go to Philadelphia . . . Right?'

I nodded.

'And you don't know what you're doing for Christmas?'

'No, I don't,' I said.

'And nor did R. And it wasn't simply that. This chap, Conte said, from what the girl told him – I believe she's Scottish – had turned into something of a fascist robot. He changed his newspaper, for instance, from the *Guardian* to the *Telegraph,* sent birthday cards to right-wing nationalists. That kind of thing. All the love, all the humanities gone, down with liberty, long live the authoritarian, up God, God bends your knees –'

'Shouldn't you open that safety valve?'

Harding let off the excess pressures and waited for the noise to subside, then smiled, apologetically: 'Sorry about that, Ranger. One gets carried away. All this government in the name of the silent majority. He was an élitist, this man Conte was writing about, Mr R, Sandra's boy-friend. Well, of course, the Communists would create monsters of the right rather than of the left. What?'

I said nothing.

'He had this peculiar obsession with cripples. Invalids. Abnormal, mutant life, deformed vegetables and so on. He had a mantelpiece full of grotesque potatoes, all cleaned and painted, double-limbed carrots and so on. Little embryo monsters, foetuses without arms, hands coming from their shoulders and that's not all. That's not all, Ranger. I'll try to find the piece. Science fiction? Jacques Conte deserves the Nobel Prize.'

'Pity he's dead.'

'He knew too much.'

'Really?'

Harding was now unscrewing the cover bolts on the kiln; the strength needed, even with a tommy-bar on the wing-nuts, seemed to go into his face and voice. 'Something big, Ranger! To do with germ warfare. Biochemical warfare.'

'I didn't know that. My son reads his stuff. Raymond didn't say anything about that. Nor did Cyril. He's a special agent. This is not what it's all about is it? Christmas and so on?'

Claude Harding sat down to rest, looked at me for a moment, speculating on my reliability. He said at last: 'You're an engineer, Ranger. I'm a scientist. Surely we know more about these things than any damned secret service – a lot of ex-policemen and soldiers and thugs. There are no secrets between people like us, surely? Scientists, physicists, chemists, technicians, mathematicians, alchemists – all working together, turning the dross into gold.'

I know this is not a very nice thing to put into a treatise, but about how I noticed that Harding while he was talking was inclined to glance at my hidden button-microphone and angle himself for best reception. I don't know how long this had been going on, but he had becoming increasingly philosophical and flowery. I mentioned that I wanted to get away early and he quickly cut it out, got on with the work.

'All I wanted to say was this, Ranger. Conte not only understood the Gdansk effect, he knew its uses. It's used not simply for programming, but also for blotting out.' He pointed his pipe at me now, his back to the gaping, steaming interior of

157

the kiln. 'There are two questions, therefore, x and y. What are you doing for Christmas *and* . . . what did you know that had to be blotted out?'

'Are you talking about me – or Mr R?'

'Frankly, I don't know,' Harding said, off-handedly. 'Jacques Conte died without naming names. His manuscripts have vanished from his Brussels apartment and Miss S has gone.'

I said: 'Perhaps she's come back to Mr R?'

'That's very unlikely. He led her a dog's life after Gdansk. She was frightened of him. He used to try and run over cripples on zebra crossings, things like that.'

I said nothing. Up and down the country cripples are getting born. The mentally and physically handicapped eating our bread, watching us. Knock them off the pavements, smash their invalid cars into ditches. Say nothing. If you happen to have brain damage, then get something to go with it, something useful, psycho-kinesis, ESP, clairvoyance, something worth while. Say nothing. The Infectious spread their filthy diseases, the Incurable take up space, the Old have no value. No farm should tolerate it. There is a great yearning for Perfection in the hard world.

'Otto Sturm thinks that you are Conte's Mr R, Ranger.'

'Oh?' I haven't seen Otto Sturm since 1944!

'So does Geoffrey Neasden,' he said then.

How the blazes do all these people from different parts of your life know each other? Or were they both at the Poly? But surely that was in the thirties? Or was it the fifties, after all? There were three images now, scan echoes, one in the Fort cockpit, one on the Poly roof and another on the beach at Nacton where I appear to be strangling somebody with a strand of seaweed.

'What you've told me is quite typical of the Gdansk effect,' said three voices in an echo-chamber.

Quite suddenly the pressures shifted. The effect of altitude on eardrums. His voice was isolated, hitting blankets, alone in my head.

'Oh?' I said again.

'Do you find that a lot of events appear to be quite coincidental?' Claude Harding was asking me.

'Yes, I do.'

'That's caused by memory gaps. According to Jacques Conte. The bits that would make them sequential are missing. Whole people are missing. There are also time-shifts and that doesn't help.'

He was beginning to frighten me. 'Does it get better?'

He tapped his Golden Virginia out on the open door of the kiln. 'I'm not entirely certain, Ranger. Of course, you'll always be slightly insane.' Scientists are so calm and factual about other people's disasters. He stooped and peered inside at the log of wood. 'I don't know whether you'd like to make a gravity check – I can chip you off a sample?'

I wanted to kill him. I wanted to kill him! I had this terrific impulse to push him right inside; close it up, quickly, twirling the big cast wing-nuts on their bolts, seal him, seal him more, start the vacuum, can't you hear it whining up, the motor, the armature relays bringing in the high amps, inverting the compressor, sucking out all the moisture, sucking out his belly, his tongue, his eyeballs, penis, anus, eardrums, sucking Claude Harding, physicist, down to less than fourteen per cent moisture content.

'Yes, I would. I would, I would,' I said. To chip me off a sample of the timber he would have to kneel into the kiln. I was trembling when he got his scalpel from the test bench. Methodically he took out a watch glass and polished it on his white coat. While he was doing this he gave me an observant smile. I forced a smile back at him. I was going to kill him. Yes, right. Lunatics kill people. He knelt into the kiln and began shaving off tiny slivers of wood so that they dropped on to the clean watch glass. No foreign bodies, no extraneous moisture. Do you remember how I tripped little Geoffrey down the steps? It was easier this time. I thrust my foot into Claude Harding's back and sent him sprawling over the log.

'Ranger!' His voice echoed the length of the steel kiln; a damp, powerless echo. He turned on his back to try to push himself out and at the same time he took a whistle from his coat pocket and blew it. Nothing came out except his breath. It gave me time to lift his feet and push them back inside, pulling the lid closed as I did so. It was as heavy as the front of a steam engine and his fingers had got their only purchase inside the flange. I could see his horror in the second it took him to make the decision whether to have his fingers amputated by the steam-proof flange or allow himself to be shut inside. He let go at the last instant and I had him – clump! The bolts came through the bosses and I swung the giant wing-nuts round on their hinged swivels, began catching the threads, a few on this bolt, a few on that, gradually sealing him in.

'Ranger! Alec! Old man! I say!'

His voice attenuated with each turn of each wing-nut as if he were screaming as he vanished down some gigantic plug-hole. It occurred to me, when I had him finally bottled, his Tom Thumb protests sounding like an educated mouse, that one could possibly make scientific use of acoustic variations. Had you thought of that? You see it was the great core of damp wood that robbed the cast-iron boiler of its natural reverberations. Just as one uses supersonic sound conductance as a flaw detector, so there must be many applications for an acoustic discriminator. Then tightening the bottom nut I found poor old Claude's whistle. He must either have thrown it at me or tried to use it to jam the door and prevent vacuum. How strange. It was a police whistle. The words Metropolitan Police and a crown stamped in the metal of the finger loop. It connected in my mind – I may be a lunatic but I'm not an idiot – with the presence of Tonne of Special Branch and his thugs outside. How delightful that a scientist of Harding's calibre had failed to make it function. I blew it myself. It worked perfectly for me. Once, twice, three times, as loudly as I could. I hoped that Harding could hear it.

'Stay where you are, Ranger.'

Tonne was standing just inside the door with a gun levelled at my head. His two male nurses came towards me, one of them holding a straitjacket.

'This is all a silly mistake,' I explained.

9

Nobody illuminates the mentally shaded too suddenly for the same reason that a sleep-walker is led back gently to his slumbers. I spent Christmas in the most beautiful surroundings. Call it a private nursing home with guards and twenty-four-hour surveillance – everyone seemed to want to be perfectly certain what I was doing for Christmas – and that would be accurate. Call it peace perfect peace, a luxury country hotel in the Surrey alps, a one-time Catholic convent, home from home; accurate, accurate, accurate. Women? Accurate. You'll find it just south of Godalming. Six acres of garden and forest, terraces, fallow deer, swimming pool.

No telephones. Bliss.

'Mr Ranger. Alec. Sorry love. Were you asleep?' This is one of the guards – Elise. Big lovely Jewish barmaid dressed in nurse's uniform two sizes too small. 'Pat's here, Dr English. Feel like seeing him? I thought I'd put some drinks in the chapel. Did you finish the wine? I'll get some up. No hurry. He's watching telly. Alec, listen. Try and find out if he's suited. I mean he could stay here tonight.'

'Come here.'

She came right into the room and I embraced her, fully, kissing into her mouth. She took hold of my penis and gave it a more or less sociable massage. 'Better put some trousers on.'

When she'd gone I dressed and went down to the chapel. There was apparently nobody there. Then I heard a voice intoning : 'And what now, my daughter?' He was sitting in the confessional, in the priest's chair, his ear to the gauze. He heard me come in and came out, smiling. 'Never resist that

when I come here. Imagine the secrets. Sister Theresa mastur-
bating in the bath again. How do you do. I'm Patrick English.'

'I am Alec Ranger.'

'Good,' he said. 'That's got that fully sorted out.'

We both laughed because we knew why we were there. He
had a Cornish face, gaunt but cheerful. His friendliness was
not professional. Forty, rich — I'd seen his Rolls outside —
expensively dressed. Completely his own man. Didn't give
much of a fuck what people thought of him.

'I started off with pigs. Animal research at Babraham.
Cambridge University. Useful background in this job. No
shit. Know what I mean? You lie to me I pass it on we go to
war — boom.'

I said : 'I'm not a spy.'

'Don't say that. Try to keep me interested.'

Elise brought some drinks in. We had a little party for half
an hour or so then she had to go. Reluctantly Patrick English
opened my file. From where I sat I could see the snow between
the pines on the opposite side of the valley; a December
afternoon sky, blue and red, above that. I was aware that he
had been reading about me and was now looking at me. I
looked at him; the Special Branch psychiatrist.

'You've had a rough time, Alec.'

I thought he was referring to the day I was brought in.
'How is Claude Harding?'

'Who? Oh, he's all right. It was a calculated risk. His job
was to drive you too far. He succeeded.'

'His job? Not another. How about my milkman? Express
Dairies. Have you got his name there? Don't I have anybody?'

'Not many,' he said, consulting the pages. 'I'll give you some
names if you want names.' He glanced up briefly. 'People who
have been helping Allied Intelligence one way or another since
Lee Oswald and Jack Ruby.' He saw my confusions. 'Since
they discovered sleepers. Seeded spies. People like you, Alec.
You all have one or two or three things in common. Amnesia.
Compulsions to violence. Élitist obsessions. Secret illusions of
Aryan grandeur. No good programming somebody to a
political assassination without giving him an ideology. Prefer-

ably a crazy one. It was cripples with you, wasn't it? Imperfection?'

As he went on a thought occurred to me. I said : 'Are you trying to incite me to murder you?'

He went quite blank for a moment; then smiled, ruefully. 'Do you know, I believe I was. Quite unintentional, love. I read too many of these bloody things.' And reading again. 'Names names names. All right, you want names. Geoffrey Neasden. His job was to take you to Tonne. Daniel Tonne. High spy number one.'

'And to his boss Ragusson. He wanted my book.'

'Not the book you're talking about, love.'

'He wanted to publish my own automation textbook – '

'Bollocks.'

'And also,' I said, with the dignity of an engineer whose life work has been slighted, 'to use my Solzhenitsyn connections in Danzig – ' Patrick English began laughing at this point and turning pages as though perhaps I was quoting some well-known hilarious fantasy which he could not quickly find. He said :

'I would never have believed it. Go on, Alec.'

He had now found the place and wanted to see if I was going to get it right. Instead I poured myself a drop more wine and lit a Dunhill. I was starting to smoke. He got the point and smiled at me.

'All that stuff was Tonne probing for CIA. They have put everyone through the grill. They did the same thing when prisoners got back from Korea. The pattern of this negative feed-back of brain rhythms is not vastly different. Amnesia, personality changes, obsessions. You may like to know that only about one sleeper in ten fulfils his assignment. Some personal crisis can halt the hypnosis or sidetrack it into something else. With you it was Sandra leaving you. If there's one thing bigger than brainbreak it is heartbreak. When they ordered her to leave you they made a bum move.'

'They ordered Sandra to leave me?'

'Yes.'

'You mean, she didn't stop loving me?'

'She still loves you, Alec.'

'She must be stark raving mad. I murdered her lover. I killed Jacques Conte. I've been working it out since I came in here. I used David Ballantine. He didn't know it. I applied negative feed-back to his brain voltages while he was asleep. Then I pointed him at Conte.'

'Marvellous,' said Dr English. 'You did the same thing to Sandra.'

'Yes, I did. How did you know that?'

'He told me.'

'Who told you?'

'Jacques Conte. I was talking to him this morning.'

'But he's dead!'

'No, no. After a time you begin to understand how espionage and counter-espionage work. You, Alec, are allowed to believe you have killed somebody. Now Special Branch has a hold on you. You will not, for instance, pop off in your lovely old Chevvy. It's outside, incidentally. We've had it overhauled and cleaned up for you – two new tyres. Let's get back to books. Ragusson wants Morag's Flying Fortress. Geoff Neasden has told him the story of your last bombing raid. Been telling it for years. Suddenly your technical book turns up and bingo – it's the skipper. You're the man to write it. When you've got your head together.'

Things were rhyming again. Relationships became clear. Motives less sinister. Innocence more sophisticated. Everybody acting dumb, waiting for me to emerge.

'I think it's coming together now, Pat. My head.'

'That's what I told Sandra this morning,' said Dr Patrick English, the MI6 psychiatrist. This man sitting opposite by the refectory table had spoken to my Scottie lassie today. Today! The same varsity voice had been in my girlie's ear. Today. It made everything possible. This moment was still valid. He said: 'She's up with her parents in Scotland. So is Conte – and his wife and kids.' He watched my face for a moment, trying to help. 'There was never anyone but you for Sandra, Alec. All your heartbreak was injected, love.'

That I could not believe. 'I saw it. In Brussels. That weekend. She was besotted with him. Once she thought I had accepted it she became hysterically affectionate.'

'Yes, she told me about that.' He tapped the book. That bloody file, I now realized, had lain in the company of everybody on the island. 'She was hysterical because she thought you were finished with her.'

'Why would she do all that to me? That terrible night she wouldn't let me sleep with her. I lay on the floor holding her foot. Coming back was a post-nuclear experience. The world was empty. If I hadn't met Cyril Dyball I wouldn't have made it.'

'He was waiting for you on the Brussels airport concourse,' Pat English said, briskly. 'Sandra phoned him from the station as soon as she had seen you off. She wanted to come after you. She wanted to kill herself.'

'Why did she do it?'

Dr English put on a Himmler voice. 'She vos unter orters. Also she wanted you cured – the old Alec.'

Now here was the great schism. Between what I did not understand and what I was beginning to understand. It had to do with time slips and three echoes and triple vision. It had to do with the Gdansk effect. Since this is an entirely subjective mental sickness there is very little chance of fighting your way out single-handed. It was English's job to know this and he knew it.

'Intelligence, i.e. Lancelot Porker, Tonne, his European oppo, NATO intelligence, CIA, they have their own methods of fighting the Gdansk effect. Waking sleepers. Triggering assassinations, sabotage. What they do is try to subject the suspect to emotional shock.'

'Why was I a suspect?'

'You were seen at Gdansk. Your photograph and prints got into records. Nobody knew you.'

'That was 1971.'

'Right.'

'Then who identified me, Patrick?'

'Daniel Tonne. The Belgian.'

'Through Geoffrey Neasden?'

'Yes.'

'Well then, you've got your arithmetic wrong, doctor.'

He clasped the big file as though I had insulted his child. I said, slowly and clearly, like Morag, God bless her and love her, like the handicapped struggling to be whole : 'Geoffrey didn't find me until Sandra had been gone nearly a year. How could Sandra have been working for MI6 if Tonne did not yet know who the hell I was?'

'Nice question, Alec. Well put. Soon you will get your ignition keys. Here it is : Tonne saw your photograph on Geoffrey's office wall.'

'What?'

'Cut from a technical journal?'

My head cleared. 'That's absolutely right. Geoff and Morag and her mother kept a scrapbook of me.'

'Not only them, Alec. You've been looked after by the survivors' club ever since you returned from Colditz.' Dimly I became aware why Morag – call her Elaine Bowen – had always been in my life. Why Jock McDonald lived underneath; popped up on Salisbury Plain when I was in trouble. Who else – Ragusson? Conte, relatives of the dead airmen we left in the wood, relatives of the dead Home Guards we left on the beach . . .

'Tell me about the flight, Skipper.'

'No.'

'Why not?'

'I don't want to.'

Dr Patrick English looked pleased. As if something had come out for him. 'You remember it clearly but you don't want to talk about it.' I nodded. He said : 'That's good. That's very good. I'll drink to that.' And when he had, he said : 'All right. I'll tell you, Skipper Ranger. You stop me if I'm wrong.' Quite unexpectedly he stood up, unzipped his flies, undid his belt, dropped his trousers around his ankles while he tucked shirt and vest into a pair of tight mauve pants. 'I like to be comfortable,' he explained. 'Too much bloody gut.' I said : 'You're wearing the pants Sandra used to buy me. Marks and Spencers. Open net fronts.' He completed his dressing. 'And what do you deduce from that, Skipper?' I told him that he was married and he was. And then he made himself comfortable with his dossier on the table and he explained me to me.

'You were not a captain. I don't want answers. There are no captains in the Air Force. Skippers, perhaps. You were known as Mad Alec. That was because of your flying, your womanizing, drinking and general irresponsibility. You could have been a squadron leader but you settled for flight lieutenant. You lost ten aircraft but all on home soil. No crews until the last one. You were then stationed at Great Gransden on the Hunts–Cambs border with an international long-range bombing squadron. There were British, Canadians and Americans in Lancasters and Forts. Your last flight was in the B–29 which is now being used as a holiday cabin in Suffolk. You took off pissed in the middle of a mess party. You took the party with you – bottles and girls. Nothing unusual about that, I'm told. Jock McDonald says it was never safe to be near a runway at take-off time. Ground crew got grabbed in the general euphoria. Your plane got hit over Düsseldorf and finally made a crash landing in what you believed to be occupied Holland or Belgium. In actual fact you had already crossed the North Sea. Had you struck south-west you were about twelve miles from Ipswich town hall. What you did, the six who were still alive – one girl, five men – was dismount a machine gun and head for the beach. Here you ran into a platoon of Dad's Army, the Home Guard, and after a brief battle you murdered the lot, believing them to be German soldiers. You then took a thirty-foot fishing boat off Dunwich beach and headed out across the North Sea, believing you were going home. Instead you were heading for Germany and you were picked up by a German vessel and ended up in the cage for the duration. After the war those of you who were sufficiently healthy and interested began looking for the wrecked plane. Neasden found it. McDonald found it. Contacts were made between the survivors and later with villagers related to the dead Home Guards. Nothing came out officially. Here is a photograph of the monument to the Home Guards on the cliff at Dunwich. The inscription attributes the massacre to enemy action. Night invaders. The only Home Guard casualties of the war. Heroes. Nobody wants to take it away from them. The villagers and the plane survivors created a conspiracy of silence. The fuselage of the B–29 was moved to a convenient bit of private beach. You are probably the only survivor who has not made use of it, Alec. It had been adapted to a six berth chalet and it's beautifully kept. There's a garden and a swimming pool. I suggested to Sandra that you meet up there. She wants you to decide. Now you can talk.'

I said : 'Who did I strangle to death?'

He said : 'Vicky's grandfather. You know Vicky. You tried to drown him but failed. Then you strangled him with a piece of seaweed. Then you were shot in the head. That's why you didn't go looking for the B–29. You knew fuck-all about it.'

'Did Sandra know about it?' I asked him.

He nodded. 'Morag told her. They needed her help.'

I said : 'Why should they keep hanging around?'

'Because you're the skipper. You never baled out on them. Geoffrey joined your night classes. Do you remember that? Early fifties?'

'I thought that was the thirties.'

He said : 'That was probably somebody else. The mind doubles up very often. Your brainwashing at Gdansk probably improved your mental condition. Even though it produced a pretty unpleasant character by all accounts.'

'You want to watch it, English,' I told him.

Elise came in. 'I've got a problem. There's a party of nuns coming here at five. Some of them used to live here. I wouldn't want them to find drinks in the chapel. All this.'

'We're through.' Pat English began gathering his things.

'You are?' Elise was disappointed. 'I was going to move you up to my apartment. You're very welcome.'

The doctor stopped packing and looked at her, fully. 'You were? I am? I will. Help me with this stuff. Let me leave you with a thought, Alec.' I think leaving me was more important than the thought. 'I don't want you to go through life wondering who you are going to assassinate or what you are going to blow up. Right; It could be much simpler than that. Consider this. The scientists at Gdansk didn't put anything into your head. They simply took something out. Erased a memory. You work in top secret establishments throughout the world. Try to remember something you shouldn't. Lead the way, Sister.'

They went out and then he came back alone and gave me my ignition keys. 'There you go,' he said.

But I didn't go. You would think wouldn't you that once I knew that Sandra loved me I would fly to her. This is not the way the heart works. I stopped worrying about her, dreaming about her, pining for the past. You would think at least we would make some communication. Besides the telephone there is the postal service and besides that we have about let us say twenty go-betweens. I am missing out David's mother who gave me all that pseudo-psychic schmuck about death and helicopters and smelling petrol. You can go off people. She was *reading* that from a new script of David's. He was not missing or in Brussels, he was there by her side prompting her. This was part of pushing Alec over the edge.

I remained in retreat. Some afternoons I talked with Sister Bridget. She was with the party of visiting nuns and my room used to be her room. She was about five feet one with a face like a smiling walnut. Probably seventy years old and bald. She had no problems. I would tell her about engineering, she would tell me about Lenny Bruce. I believed she identified with his Aunt Mema. She brought the Berkeley concert album and his autobiography and she always took them away again. I would have to read it in little bits. If you remember his mother and his aunt, 'a little old bald lady', were always claiming that men had been flashing at them from the bushes. I think it is side three. Sister Bridget used to play side three a lot. All that stuff about the Pope. It was this and his book that started me writing this diary. I mean more than a psychiatrist's request you need a belly urge.

Moosh died. The afternoons came to an end. It is always afternoon at Mulberry Hill. This is as close as I can tell you the name of the place. It doesn't need tourists. Sometimes the afternoons in a place like that last all day and all night. Your first drink lies comfortably ahead. If there were guards there they were cleverly disguised as cheerful local people doing the cleaning. For a time I played draughts in the chapel with a man who wore handcuffs. He would shift his pieces with both hands, refusing to be helped. If you heard shots in the night, later there would be pheasant or venison on the silver tray. Prisons run like this would be full. What I got the strong impression was that espionage is an upper-class thing. And then Elise came in with the bad news. I had thought that the poodle was being looked after by Morag and Geoffrey at Wembley. All this time, Christmas to February, she had been with Sandra at Chalk Farm, waiting for daddy to decide to come home.

No more Al'k! It took some time to absorb. Remember that long walk round the Cornish coast from Portreath to the dunes of Hayle. We started out blackberrying. The red streams and the derelict mines and the glimpses of ocean and coasters in dips in the land. And then we had to take turns carrying the dog. 'We shall sell you and buy a real doggie!' Sandra would tell her.

Nice to think they had been together these few weeks; my four-legged ambassador with her anal glands beginning to pong, her heart needing tablets and drugs to fight her flea allergies. Moosh was really a very old person. Our relationship, mine and Sandra's, had been her whole existence in the hard world. And now it was over.

I saw the body. In my head.

Ping went my heart. My last flying fortress, my tin heart, had crashed. Elise had been listening as I told her in as casual a way as possible about Moosh and suddenly I could not go on. The Jewish girl watched my tears with some sort of concealed relief; as if, perhaps, her job was over.

10

Fasten your safety belts; we are on the home beam. I don't want to worry you but there are about ten possible landings. I drive home to Chalk Farm and Sandra is sitting knitting me a woolly. Or I arrive and the place is in darkness. Jock is in the bar of the Barge. He tells me that Sandra took the museum up to Oxfam in Gayton Road and took a train down to Cornwall. I find her on the beach at Portreath. Sleep together in the apartment at the top of the stone steps. That's not very good. I never visualize a sexual reunion. That is very unimportant. I would rather screw Vicky and Morag and Janet and Elise and Jeni Thirshall and keep Sandra McPherson for walking towards on the beach.

'How's your little doggie?' This is one of the best ones. I have driven the long dark February roads from Surrey to Chalk Farm. I have arrived in the bar of the Barge at secretary coming home time. I have two stools and two drinks. Scotch and dry for me, brandy and Babycham for Sandra. I can't get close enough to the window to watch the tube station entrance. I have to stand on tiptoe and look through somebody's conversation. 'I was at a Burns' night. I met this man Schneider who knew you.' 'I remember Schneider. How's he getting on?' The trains empty about every two minutes and people disperse under the yellow lamplight. Suddenly there is this little woollen head. It's going the wrong way. She does not know I am here. I rush out and run after her, flapping up the path and across the road, ignoring the traffic, like the night Cyril and David and I ran back to look for her. All my dreams are brought together in this panic hunt, like a dog race without a hare. The smells and the visions and the logics are all in place but there is no Sandra. Then all at once the whistle – the cheerful musical third.

'Alec?'

'Sandra!'

I have run past her and she is waiting for me to go back. She has put her parcels down on the ground. I walk back to her and it is Sandra. What do we say now? Her nose is the same length. A bit pink at the end in the cold. Her beautiful Scottish eyes are fluttering at me. All these landings are in my head as I sit in Mulberry Hill with my nurse holding my hand.

'Did you kill her, Alec?'

'Yes,' I said.

'Do you want to take us with you?'

The voices are the voices of the rescue team. Raymond is there calling me dad. Cyril Dyball and David are there. We travel in the black-windowed Citroen ambulance. The huts are at the end of a long-disused coal line between Erith in Kent and the river. In the frozen winter of 1947 we conducted a kiln drying and timber impregnation programme there. The weekend Sandra came back to fetch her winter things because she was getting cold in Brussels, I took her to the derelict hutment on the way to Dover ferry.

'No need to go in, mate,' said Det. Superintendant Dyball. 'She's not there now.' When I shut Claude Harding in the kiln they checked back on every kiln operation I had ever been associated with. Including Bovril's fencing-timber works in the Argentine. That was the hot summer of 1959. I said to David: 'Was there a funeral?' I could see it at the dead centre, as Sandra always called it, in Lairg. Everybody attending, my crew, my island. I could see Sandra lying in the rusty boiler taking weeks to die because it was no longer airtight. I could see myself sitting in Broadmoor getting it all on to paper. They call me the Engineer. A certain social status goes with it. Better than Mad Alec. In the evenings I play draughts with that same man in handcuffs. His name is Martin. He killed and ate his next-door neighbour's baby.

'What did *you* do, Alec?' he asks me, between moves.

'I strangled a man. I was shot through the head. I was electrically brainwashed by the Russians. I killed my girl-friend.'

'Your move,' he said.

But I was suddenly seeing babies in jars. I dreamed the following rhyme:

> One step nearer the grave my friend,
> One step closer to hell.
> What the young man saw when he opened the door
> And the doctor began to wave:
> Get back, get back, get back, my friend;
> This is the end, the end my friend,
> A babe in arms without any arms
> And a hand coming out of its neck, my friend,
> And its twin with one leg as round as an egg
> And its brain exposed to the air, dear God.
> Its brain instead of its hair, dear God,
> And a wink's as good as a nod, poor sod,
> For they'll drop like peas in a pod.
> From the bellies of women and fall like frogs
> And they'll give the remains to the dogs, young man,
> Is what the doctor cried. . . .

There was more than this for it went on and on but this was as much as I could write down in my engineering day book, still half asleep, still envisioning words and image mixed together. A laboratory in East Germany that I entered by mistake. When I awoke in the bright morning between the clean sheets with the blessed sun-touched pines outside the window, Elise was reading my night scrawl.

'What does this mean?'

I said: 'It means the last piece of my head has come together.' I knew why I was directed to Gdansk. The place I had been working at was part of a Russian biological warfare research establishment. I said: 'What has happened to Martin?' She said: 'Who is Martin?' I said: 'The man in handcuffs.' She said: 'That's Peter Renbro. We had to stop him scratching himself. He's gone home. You have been dreaming, Alec. What do you want to do? Here is Sandra's office address and number – it was in the post.'

She handed me a piece of blue notepaper (how do people use the same blue notepaper all their lives?) and there was my Scottie girl's handwriting.

Dear Alec,
Here is my address, 9 till 6 : Champion Rugs, 6, High Holborn, London W.C.1. Tel : 837 7011.

Love and cheepers :
Sandra. XXX

I looked at it for a long time. So casual it was. Something poetic would have been more acceptable. I said : 'What made you open it?' Elise said : 'I have to open everything. But with most other residents I steam and close it. We don't have any secrets, do we?' She was openly confiscating my poem. Now I looked into Elise's eyes. Stopped being superficial. I said : 'Is my dog dead?' She nodded. I said : 'I thought that was to soften me up?' She shook her head. Then she said : 'But it did. You cried. Then we slept together.' I said : 'Did you give me any dope?' She said : 'Every night. I have my orders. You have completed the cycle.' I said : 'What is this place?' She said : 'A home for tired spies.' (I am an engineer! I am an engineer! A million interrogations.) I said : 'Was I a spy?' She nodded again. Then she said : 'Are you going to telephone Sandra?'

The telephone, you understand, was hidden away in the confessional. The troubles and the confusions and the uncertainties were thinning down, lies turning into the ultimate truth. I sit in the confessional, my head bowed to the bronze gauze, the white earpiece to my ear.

'Sandra?'
'Champion Rugs. Good morning.'
'Can I speak to Miss McPherson, please.' One should say 'May I'. One realizes a shade too late.
'I'm putting you through.'
'Hulloo?' Musical third.

'Sandra?'

'Yes. Who is that?'

'Alec.'

'Alec Ranger?'

'Sandra. Are you all right? I've been terrified of this moment. I don't know which would be worse. This or meeting you face to –'

'Alec, can you hold on a moment? Mr Watson, there's been a call for you. There are some patterns coming doon from the Bradford works. They're to be collected at King's Cross after twelve o'clock noon. . . .'

It was always thus. At the end of the equation, x equals love and love is in the head.